Reviews

An absolute gem of a book. At first glance it appears to be a crime or
whodunit novel, and it does have elements of that in it. But it is so much
more. It explores loyalty and friendship within families, with friends
and colleagues, and lovers. It looks at homelessness in a thoughtful and
compassionate way. And it considers the ethics of truth and raises the
question whether it is ever justifiable to lie or to conceal the truth. The
characters are all fully rounded, and it is a mark of the writer's skill that
everyone is portrayed with affection and empathy, from High Court judges
and homeless people to detective constables and high profile actors. Ginny
Davis has personal experience of the backstage of court rooms through her
work as a barrister. She is also a highly successful playwright and performer.
This unusual combination of backgrounds added to meticulous location
research makes for a totally convincing and authentic novel. Although it deals
with some uneasy issues, it is ultimately a gripping and heart-warming read.

Delyth Jenkins (Author - *That Would be Telyn*)

Quite a page-turner. Explores issues of truth-telling in a very accessible and
stimulating way. What could be more important?

Christopher Lamb

The plot was genius, lots of interesting intertwining of life and its absurdity
and how different personality types bounce off each other, causing all sorts
of tweaks and nicks of pain and pleasure. The tension is tightly wound right
through the book and superbly resolved. I was captivated. Interesting side
activity and personalities ground the journey towards the very enjoyable end.

Philippa Dearsley

I cannot emphasise enough how much I enjoyed reading it. I have actually
read it twice - I read it too quickly the first time as I just couldn't put it down -
I kept thinking, "I must know what happens next".

J Dodds

WHAT LIES BENEATH THE SURFACE

Publisher: Independent Publishing Network

Publication date: January 2021

ISBN 978-1-80049-336-0

Text © Ginny Davis

First published 2020

Second edition 2021

All rights reserved

Please direct all enquiries to the author

info@ginnydavis.com
www.ginnydavis.com

For Mum

THE REGENT'S CANAL

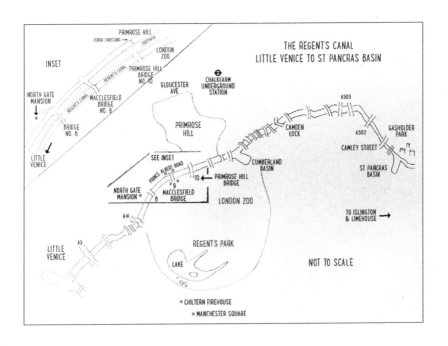

THURSDAY 4th APRIL 2019

REGENT'S CANAL – BETWEEN BRIDGE NO. 9 AND PRIMROSE HILL
BRIDGE

11:50pm

Davey died in the Regent's Canal. He was forty-three.
  At an earlier time in his life, when the odds had been against him, he had
expected to die young. But when the moment came, he did not have time
to consider the irony that he was now living in comparative safety. To his
knowledge, he had few enemies, and those of whom he was aware carried
neither arms nor weaponry. He took few risks, passing his time peacefully and
mostly unnoticed by the busy people amongst whom he occupied space. But
these things happen.
  He died near to Bridge No. 9, named Macclesfield Bridge, nicknamed 'The
Blow-Up Bridge' after an accident in 1874 in which gunpowder exploded on a
barge travelling to a quarry in the Midlands. The bridge links the busy Prince
Albert Road in St John's Wood to Regent's Park, London.
  The water beneath is shallow and its surface lies a good eighteen inches
below the level of concrete kerb stones. A young, fit man would easily be able
to climb out of the water if he toppled in for some reason.
  Four and a half hours earlier Davey had lain on his side. Unconscious?
No. Conscious then? Barely. Asleep? No. Drugged? Yes, spice. Drunk? Only
a little. His head rested on blue brick paving stones, not his first choice of
pillow. He had thrown a punch at the man's head then flailed defensively,
hopefully, uselessly. A body blow to his diaphragm winded him badly. He
bent gasping "Stop. All right?" Then a shove. He stumbled sideways, unable
to counterbalance his weight and threw out a hand to break his fall. A snap.
Sharp, unmitigated pain shot like electricity around his wrist. "Fucking shite!"
He closed his eyes and waited for the kicking. Nothing. Then a presence close
by. Scent of perfume. Female. A male voice said urgently, "Come on, leave him.
Quick. Run!" He heard footsteps running. Then silence. He had no idea how
long he lay there. Thirty seconds, forty, an hour? Oblivion.
  Later her voice. Soft, Irish, concerned. "Davey love, you're hurt."

BETWEEN THE ROYAL COURTS OF JUSTICE AND MANCHESTER SQUARE, MARYLEBONE

LATE AFTERNOON

Gray usually enjoyed his walk home. He had a choice of route. Tonight, he had needed to think so he had left the Royal Courts of Justice by the back door onto Carey Street, skirted the tennis courts and lawns of Lincoln's Inn Fields and taken quiet roads home to Manchester Square, Marylebone through Bloomsbury and Fitzrovia.

Throughout the day, he had grown increasingly annoyed with himself for having forwarded an email. It was not particularly unusual for misdirected messages to land in his inbox. Inadvertently sending an email to the wrong addressee is easily done when the sender's mind is busy. Nevertheless, whenever they arrived, he would be mildly surprised that lawyers and even fellow High Court judges could be so careless. When the intended recipient was clear, he would forward the message on, in a spirit of efficiency.

Just after lunch today, seated at his desk surrounded by books, papers, files and all the trappings of senior judicial office, he was immersed in checking through a judgment he had just completed when a message from Patrick Kingdom QC arrived. It began "Gracia, Let yourself in." So, he had ping'd it on to the only Gracia he knew. Then he had had a second thought, read the message through in full and tried frantically and hopelessly to find a way of dragging it back. What a stupid, stupid thing to do! The fool that he was! During the walk home he had debated with himself whether he should email Patrick. Or Gracia? Or ring? By the time he had reached his front door he had resolved to do none of this. It might only make matters worse. He hoped that neither of them would mention the matter to him again and that they all would be able to pretend the mistake had never been made. "Least said," he told himself. But he was not convinced.

GLOUCESTER AVENUE, PRIMROSE HILL

MID AFTERNOON

Gracia took off her glasses and placed them beside her laptop. She scrunched her eyes, rolled her shoulders back and around and stretched each side of her neck. She was seated at the pine desk she had bought on impulse from a charity shop ten years ago during a visit to the Cotswolds. She opened her eyes and slowly they adjusted to the view from her window over neglected neighbouring gardens. At a first glance it might have seemed to an onlooker that her own flat was similarly chaotic, but each artefact had been carefully chosen and put in place, from the Japanese parasol hanging in the corner of the room, to the rag rug on the floor in front of the Victorian fireplace and the lengths of Italian lace which waved at the windows whenever they were left open. She had moved to Primrose Hill shortly before she bought the table and the area suited her well. Just around the corner a choice of vintage and designer shops was squeezed between informal, welcoming cafes and privately run convenience stores which stayed open till late. Ten minutes walk to the top of Primrose Hill and she could breathe in deeply and look out over London. Fifteen, and she was on the Regent's Canal. Less than twenty to Regent's Park.

So deep was her concentration on a new script that she had completely lost track of time. Ratings for the first series of *Initiate* on Netflix had prompted a second. The producers wanted to put her character, Annie, at the centre of a new storyline but Gracia had almost blown her prospects early one Sunday morning, shortly before the contract had been finalised, when she was snapped throwing up in Oxford Street. The lucky photographer had sold the picture for a five-figure sum. Fortunately for Gracia, most of the following day's tabloids covered a far bigger story about the Royal Family, but someone from the production company of *Initiate* found her story online.

"This is bad, Gracia," her agent had told her. "They are really pissed off. I've had to promise you'll keep your nose clean from now on. When the public see you, they are looking at Annie. She doesn't throw her guts up all over central London after a night out. I've pulled them back on board but promise me it won't happen again." Gracia had promised; contracts for the second series were signed and six weeks of filming in Liverpool and Romania was due to begin in ten days.

Gracia had spent this day examining the role of Annie in detail, making notes on how other characters relate to her and she to them, each in turn, in order to create a three-dimensional image. She lifted her phone to check the time and found several new messages. She scrolled through those with which she need not concern herself. But there was an email from Gray which had arrived just after lunch.

Graham Andrew
To: Gracia Peel
Was this for you?
Forwarded message from Patrick Kingdom
Date: 4th April 2019
Subject: Tonight
To: Graham Andrew <Graham.Andrew@hotmail.com>

Gracia, Let yourself in. I'll be back at 6:15pm. Veuve Clicquot in the fridge. Between my sheets you'll find a new nightie. Put it on. Take it off at 6:14pm. Patrick xxxx

Gray.

Horrified, she stood up, swore and threw the phone onto the patchwork covered sofa beside her, then picked it up to read Patrick's message again.

Even as she dialled his number, she knew he was probably in court and unable to answer.

"Darling." His voice held an easy, pleasant tone. "What a nice surprise!"

She cut him short. "You realise what you've done?"

"No. What?"

"You only sent your stupid email to Gray instead of me."

Pause.

"Fuck."

"Quite."

"How do you know?"

Anger rendered her incapable of relating any more than the bare fact. "He forwarded it to me."

"Gracia, I'm so sorry."

"Well, that doesn't exactly help, does it? Forget the champagne and your stupid nightie. I'll be at yours at six."

She had deliberately forced him to return home fifteen minutes earlier than he had planned. For the rest of the afternoon, she raged and achieved nothing useful, restlessness and inability to concentrate only increasing her anger. All she could think of was Patrick's stupidity and Gray's likely reaction. At 5:15pm she had a shower and got dressed.

Having buttoned her dress, she looked at her reflection in the gilt-framed boudoir mirror that stood in the corner of her bedroom. Front. OK. Actually, more than OK. The dress was new. Mediterranean blue cotton embossed with tiny indigo tigers, mid-waisted, long-sleeved, calf length. It felt right for the occasion and she knew that she would probably never want to wear it again. She left the top two buttons unfastened, re-considered the second one down and did it up again. Then she stood, square on, hands on hips, pushed the sleeves up to three quarter length and appraised the effect. Too business-like. She pulled them back down again. Then her eyes moved down to her feet. Black leather boots. Wrong for the lightweight dress but she planned to walk to Patrick's flat and they were comfortable. In any case, she was hardly aiming to make an impression. Leave one, more like. Neither of them was going to be thinking about what she had on her feet.

"You're just as much to blame," she tried telling herself, but her brain wasn't having it.

She turned for a side-on look at the figure that had been recognised and exploited by paparazzi and tabloids since the success of the first series of *Initiate*, then turned around and looked over her shoulder, wondering again why she even cared about her appearance. "Because," she answered, "if this is going to be the last look he gets at me, it's going to be unforgettable." It was. The A-line cut perfectly shaped her hips. She picked up her black jacket, bag and keys, slung the jacket over her shoulder and headed for the door.

"Shit. Nearly forgot." She returned to the bedroom and opened her wardrobe. From the top shelf she grabbed a black-fringed wig. He hated it. Serve him right. She wound her own wavy, blonde hair into a knot on the top of her head and pulled the wig over it, checking the mirror to make sure that the fringe was straight. Sunglasses? Outside the window the sun was invisible behind a blanket of dank cloud. Disguise, rather than protection from UV rays would have been the point of wearing them. But still, she decided not to bother. It was annoying not being able to see properly on a dull day and she was pissed off enough already.

Slamming the front door behind her, she strode out onto Gloucester Avenue then turned left, passing her favourite shops with too much annoyance to allow a glance in at the windows, then marched at a pace driven by unsuppressed rage alongside Primrose Hill towards the Regent's Canal whose path led almost to Patrick's door.

Why were men always so bloody stupid?

TOP FLOOR FLAT, NORTH GATE MANSION BLOCK, ST JOHN'S WOOD

5:45pm

"How's Bunter?" Patrick took a glass from his kitchen cupboard, placed it on the worktop and opened the fridge for gin and a can of tonic water. He lodged the phone between his chin and left shoulder in order to be able to mix his drink.

Patrick's wife, Jenny, lived in Northamptonshire with Bunter and his brother, Billy. Bunter had torn his ear charging through a barbed wire fence in pursuit of a rabbit. He was not the brightest of dogs.

Patrick poured himself a generous two inches of gin, then held the tonic can at the furthest reach from the phone so that Jenny would not hear a give-away snap and fizz when he opened it. He watched the liquid bubble and settle within the glass as he listened to Jenny describe the wound and tell him that Bunter snapped at her hand every time she tried to bathe his ear with salt water. She was worried that the wound would become infected and did not know if dogs could contract tetanus.

"So, I can't decide whether or not to take him to the vet. What do you think?" she asked, anxiously.

"Why not leave it twenty-four hours? See how it looks then?" Patrick took a sip of his drink and realised he'd forgotten to add ice and a slice of cucumber.

She sounded relieved.

"Yes, you're right. I will. All OK there?"

He told her everything was fine. The trial he had been prosecuting for the past six weeks had concluded with convictions all round.

"Well done, darling. When will you be home?"

"Tomorrow. I'll be there by teatime. A few things to tidy up here before the weekend. OK?"

"Course. You should have an early night and get some sleep. You've worked hard on this one. What do you think swung the jury?" It was good of her to ask. He knew that she rarely understood the minutiae of his work.

"Let's talk about it tomorrow, OK?"

He wanted the call to end, not only in order to have both hands free to attend to his drink but to give himself time to think clearly about what was about to happen.

It is often thought that the skill of the criminal barrister is the ability to think on one's feet. So it is. But it is not one he or she likes to employ. The key to success is more mundane: preparation, thorough preparation for what might appear to others to come as a surprise. Every question has a purpose and its own place in the choreography of defence or prosecution. Only ever ask questions to which you already know the answer is the barrister's mantra. Thinking on your feet is the last resort.

Patrick had built up a strong criminal practice litigating all manner of wrongdoing and paying close attention to human behaviour, in particular the motivations which drive criminals to deviate from the lawful path chosen by respectable citizens. He was an expert in human understanding and already he had a pretty clear idea of how Gracia was feeling. He wished to be prepared with the right reaction when she arrived. What that reaction should be would take some thought.

5:50pm

Jenny Kingdom put her phone down on the kitchen island then lowered her glasses from her head and leant onto her elbows to read the recipe book she had opened earlier. Beside her was a pen and notebook jauntily entitled *Shopping Lists.* She began to write.

Dried fruit
Sugar
Brandy
Butter
Eggs
Flour
Cinnamon
Nutmeg
Marzipan

She paused to consider. Should she make her own marzipan or buy ready-made? The family was going to be together in a couple of weeks for Easter and simnel cake was a traditional must. Ready-made marzipan was very tempting. Provided there were the requisite number of little balls to represent the twelve disciples, the men in her life would not be particular about how the marzipan tasted. Was it twelve balls on a simnel cake or eleven? She could not remember whether or not Judas was conventionally omitted. Or was it thirteen? She would have to look it up. But ready-made? No, she could not allow herself to sink so low. She added ground almonds and icing sugar to her list.

She was excited that everyone was coming home. They hadn't been all together since Christmas. She would have liked their family gatherings to have taken place more often but always hesitated to suggest too many. The boys were grown up and settled into their own lives now, after all.

The kitchen island had once been the hub of the home. The oak structure was now dated but when they had had it installed it was state of the art. When the family were all living at home the island had been loaded with notes from school, letters to answer, the newspapers, invitations, flyers from local businesses and all the this and that of everyday life. In the evenings and at weekends Patrick would lean against it and chat while she cooked, and Rob and Charlie mucked around on the Nintendo in the TV room next door. Nowadays the granite surface was empty and clean. Kew pots filled with orchids occupied the spaces left vacant by family clutter.

Theirs was a handsome, brick built, ivy clad Georgian property originally owned by a prosperous Northampton shoe manufacturer who had hoped that it would remain in his family for future generations. He, unfortunately, had only been able to father one child, a girl who had emigrated to Canada. Neither she nor her husband saw any financial advantage in owning a large house in a distant country and so it was sold.

Each of the several owners who had since had custody of the property had made his mark on it in one way or another – the lawyer who had widened the doors and built an extension to house his library, the surgeon who had converted the extension into a kitchen and graced the front entrance with matching stone columns, and the accountant who had built garages for his collection of classic cars but had been forced to sell, having taken ill-considered risks on the stock market and lost everything. Patrick had chanced upon the For Sale board planted in the verge beside the entrance to the drive one day when his trial in Northampton Crown Court had gone short. He was a junior barrister, not long married, and, with time on his hands, he had taken a circuitous route home to Oxford through the villages.

"Shut your eyes," he told Jenny the following Sunday as they approached in her Morris Minor.

"I can't. I'm driving." She laughed.

"OK. Pull in here. We'll walk."

Jenny obeyed. "What are we doing?" she asked as she got out of the car.

The house sat in grounds at the end of a drive which lay around a bend.

"Now shut your eyes." He took her hand and guided her to the end of the drive. "Open them."

Jenny looked around. "Where are we?"

"How would you like to live there?"

Her eyes followed his to the elegant edifice and she laughed again. "Very much. Does it come with a butler? Grooms? A nice housekeeper in a starched pinny with one of those things on her head? Because I'd always insist on staff. You do understand that?"

Patrick was too excited to join in with the joke.

"I mean it. It'd be a risk but I've had a word with a financial advisor and as long as my practice doesn't fall apart, it's manageable. What do you think? Would you be OK living here? I mean it would not be like living in Oxford. We'd be a bit out of the way. You might have to move office?"

"I don't know Patrick. I mean what if my wellies got dirty walking across all these fields. I'd hate that." Jenny's face was dead straight.

Patrick looked crestfallen.

"You silly chump! Of course, I'd be OK. OK? Are you joking? It's beautiful!"

Now they had lived there for nigh on three decades. She and Patrick had occasionally discussed downsizing after the boys moved out, but the house held memories of family life that were too precious for Jenny to abandon.

"Plus", she had countered to Patrick's suggestion that downsizing had economic advantages, "when the boys marry and have their own families we'll need all this space."

Neither boy was showing any signs of settling down to a permanent relationship, let alone children. It didn't matter. With Patrick working away most weeks Jenny could confine her activity to just a few rooms. The remainder lay cold and dusty, waiting for the boys and their imaginary wives and children.

"Do you get lonely?" her best friend had asked.

"Heavens no, I don't have time," she had replied.

A comfortable routine gradually replaced the dashing about she had done to ferry the boys here and there as they grew up. Morning dog walking and then the middle part of the day in which to potter, sometimes in the garden, sometimes shopping, one afternoon a week ferrying supplies for the local foodbank. Book club and bridge evenings gave her a midweek social life.

When Patrick's London practice grew buoyant, he rented a flat in St John's Wood and so began the weekly commuting: leaving after supper on Sunday and returning home early on Friday evening. Occasionally Jenny's routine would be broken by Patrick working from home during the week, though that had not been his practice of late. But he always came back at weekends. She had the dogs to look after so, as a rule, they did not see each other from Monday to Friday.

She was proud of him. He had taken silk in his mid-forties which, she understood, was good going for a criminal barrister. A natural storyteller, he would hold everyone's attention at dinner parties with vivid accounts of crime. Female friends would listen agog when his tales involved sexual deviation and wrongdoing, their partners happy to let him titillate their wives and girlfriends in the hope that it might be a prelude to their turn for arousal later on. Jenny focused on providing delicious and healthy food and didn't compete. The team effort made them popular hosts. Girlfriends spoke enviously of the Kingdoms' living arrangements saying they reckoned they could probably put up with their husbands too if they weren't there the whole bloody time.

"But aren't you worried?" asked the closest friend with genuine concern, emboldened by a glass or two of wine, "about him being all on his own in London with nothing to do in the evenings? He's a good-looking man, Jenny."

"He wouldn't be so stupid." She thought for a moment. "And if he was, I'd just have to hope he'd have the sense to keep quiet about it."

Rosie had said to meet her here. She had not arrived yet but Davey knew she would come. Whenever Rosie said she would do something, she did it. He had teased her about it once. They had been sitting on a patch of grass near the Mansion House. How long ago? A year maybe.

"So, Rosie Sheehan, how is it you always turn up where you say you'll be?" He had asked as a joking accusation. "Because round these parts that is not behaviour we expect."

"Well, Davey," she replied. "When I was a little girl me Da would beat me if I didn't keep my promises."

Davey was not sure what she was telling him but felt safer keeping the tone lighthearted.

"The bastard. I would beat him now, I would, if he laid a hand on you."

She had shaken her head. "Oh, I don't think you would, Davey. He was a big man, me Da."

Davey had set aside his bottle of cider and stood up, raising himself unsteadily to full height, then onto his tip toes to add an inch or so. He wanted to make her smile and succeeded as he tottered uncertainly before her.

"Are you saying he was bigger than me, Rosie Sheehan?"

"I am afraid I am saying that, yes I am. He was quite a giant."

"But you are not a giant, Rosie Sheehan?"

When they were both standing, she was chest height to Davey and he was no giant either.

"That would be because I take after me Ma. She was only five foot two in her heels. So was I, last time I checked."

Davey had laughed. They had known each other for a week or so and there was something intriguing about this girl from his side of the water. He wanted to know more. He kept up his jokey tone.

"Sure though, did you have no brothers, to stand up to the giant?"

"No, there was only me and me Ma but, as I say, she was a midget." Her expression became sad. "Turned out me Da was not quite the gentleman when it came to midgets."

"Oh?"

Rosie plucked at a blade of grass.

"And when he threatened me with the breadknife, she decided it was time for us to go away and make a new life but unfortunately that was not possible because then she died."

The jokiness was over.

"Oh Rosie," he said. "How old were you?"

"Fifteen. We came across the water so he couldn't find us. She had a friend in Essex who took us in. But Ma got really poorly, and there was nothing could be done. And when she died her friend didn't want me around anymore. Because her husband did, if you understand what I mean?"

"Rosie love." He put his arm around her and held out his bottle. "Have some of this."

She shook her head. "I'm all right. It was a long time ago."

"How long, Rosie?"

He enjoyed looking at her face but found it impossible to tell how old she might be. Rough living had taken its toll on her skin which was sun-damaged and lined. Her hair was bleached and long. Her grey eyes spoke no innocence but had not lost their light. He raised one of her hands in his and smoothed the back. A suggestion of plumpness covered her knuckles. He reckoned she might still be under thirty-five.

She sidestepped the question. "I haven't been counting."

He had been tempted to ask more. Had she lived rough ever since then? If he was right about her age then twenty years was a long time for such a lifestyle. Even he knew that, and he was relatively new to it. Had she been in serious relationships? Had children? But the questions could wait, and he did not need the answers. She had a story and a history. So did everyone. More importantly she had a life that, for whatever reason, she regarded as worth living. She was company, and she made him happy. What more was there?

They had never agreed that they were 'going out' as such. For two people who were already outdoors virtually all the time the expression was ironically inappropriate. But naturally they had gravitated towards each other and now they rarely separated. Rosie had taught him how to be safe and where to seek shelter in a world which could not be protected by lock and key. Gradually he had learned the answers to the questions he did not ask that day. Had she lived rough ever since? "On and off." Relationships? "How long have you got, Davey?" she had quipped. Children? "Maybe one day," she hoped. Was she ever lonely? "Sure. It can be lonely, this life. But take each day as it comes, right?"

He looked around to check that he was at the right bridge. A little black and white plaque told him this was Bridge No. 9. Where was her note? He pushed his hand into his trouser pocket to feel around. Crumbs and rubbish parted to make way for his stained fingers. Nothing there. He tried the inside pocket of his anorak. Here! A piece of paper. 'Regent's Canal Bridge No. 9 xx'

He folded and replaced it, tired now. It had been a long walk westwards, so he climbed up a concrete slope under the north arch of the bridge to lie down to sleep for a while.

MANCHESTER SQUARE, MARYLEBONE
EARLY EVENING

"You should come over some time. It's a laff, you know. We put the music on, have a dance. There's always sweets and crisps. Pizza and pop tonight. Why don't you come? My name's Annie, by the way."

Gracia smiled invitingly. Her legs, wrapped in high-waisted, skin-tight, ripped-knee jeans, straddled a city centre planked bench. She wore a short-sleeved polo neck crop top and thick soled trainers. Her face was made up to take ten years off her actual age. Glossy lips. Cheeks shiny with cheap foundation. Broad licks of liquorice liner framed her eyes which exuded friendship and temptation. The girls sitting opposite her were wearing school uniform.

Gray's stomach rumbled. He glanced away from the TV to drank down a fistful of cashews with a mouthful of Margaux and then replaced the glass on a round Georgian oak side table and returned to *Initiate*.

"All right," smiled one of the schoolgirls cheekily, a lively-eyed redhead whose overall manner and body language indicated attitude. *"Sounds great. Beats arguing with me step-dad. Shall we?"* She turned to her companion. The second girl appeared less assured. She was tall and her school skirt was rolled over at the waist, revealing boyishly long, straight legs. Her eyes were wide and innocent. Chewed fingernails twiddled a fluffy pink tag which was attached to her school bag. She looked doubtful.

"I can't, I'm supposed to look after my sister." She turned to the redhead. *"You said you'd come to mine."* The redhead looked crestfallen.

Gracia nodded in understanding. *"Aw shame. How old is she? How old are you two actually, sorry, I never asked."*

"Sixteen," the redhead hastily boasted.

Her friend looked at her in surprise, then added, *"And Sian's eleven."*

Gracia's eyes lit up. *"Tell you what. Bring her along too. She'll have a great time!"*

Gray couldn't be objective. To him Gracia's portrayal of Annie in *Initiate* was perfect. He knew he was biased. He had cared for her from the minute he was informed that she had become an orphan. His twin sister, who had adored him so much as to devise for her only child a feminine name as close as possible to Gray with a hint of the Latin for "gratitude", had died, together with their parents and her husband, in a helicopter crash on their way back from a wedding on St Mary's, Isles of Scilly. Gracia had been staying with a schoolfriend for the weekend. Her sole surviving relatives were her paternal grandmother, a widow who lived with worsening vascular dementia as her sole companion, and Gray. Gracia was his goddaughter. Decision made. She was eleven years old. He was forty.

"Right. 11a Ranulf Road. It's behind the Shell Garage, know it?" The schoolgirls nodded and the redhead put the address in her phone as Annie continued. *"Any time after half five. Oh, and dress up if you want to. We usually do."* With a cheery *"See you later then?"* the girls giggled off toward the bus stops. Annie watched them go and dialled a number. *"Hi, Daz. Three more tonight. Two say they are sixteen but they're obviously younger, fourteen, maybe. One's got to bring her little sister. She's eleven. It's the only way they could come. But for a first night I thought it'd be all right. Anyway, reckon there another half hour's worth here till the school kids are out of town, then I'm done."*

Gray's elegant townhouse flat comprised two storeys divided by a wide, mahogany bannistered staircase in an attractive square just south of Marylebone High Street. He had bought the lower floor early on in his career at the Bar with fingers crossed that he would be able to keep up the mortgage payments. When Gracia's parents died he had rented it out and moved into her family home in Clapham, believing that she needed the consistency of continuing to live at home. But the arrangement was unsuccessful. His bedroom was always described by Gracia as 'Mummy and Daddy's room' as if he were a temporary guest outstaying his welcome. One day he had suggested that the rotting garden shed be replaced. "But it's Daddy's shed," she had protested, bursting into tears. And so it became clear to Gray that Gracia's passage to adjusting to the loss of her parents was not eased but inhibited by her insistence that nothing in the house could ever change. It had become a shrine. So, a couple of years later when the apartment above Gray's in Manchester Square went on the market, he bought it and converted the two into one, providing ample space upstairs for three bedrooms and bathrooms. With the promise of her own private bathroom, Gracia had agreed to the move but, on the day they left Clapham, she had cried unconsolably and in every room left little envelopes containing farewell messages.

The room in which he now sat was on the lower floor. It served as both snug and study depending on his reason for being there. After Gracia had moved out, he had had it furnished and decorated in gentleman's residence style under the guidance of a pleasant but expensive interior designer. In front of the sash window overlooking the Square stood his large oak, brass-handled desk at which, to the distant underscore of residential life within the capital – far-off sirens, occasional voices, a car door shutting or wheels on tarmac – he would sit to write, do personal admin and handle emergency applications to the High Court when he was the designated judge for overnight or weekend duty.

Usually, as on this occasion, the room served as his snug. Two large, amber and maroon loose-covered armchairs sat either side of a patterned Indian rug on which stood a large upholstered stool in complementary colours. The TV was in the opposite corner. Beside it were bookshelves piled with novels and books on art history.

Framed photographs on a side table included one taken in Cambridge shortly before Gracia was born. The colours were faded by sunlight but anyone who cared to peer would see a younger Gray, as a barrister whose irregular hours allowed time to teach civil procedure part-time at Trinity Hall, his former College. His hair, now thin and grey was then thick and dark. Heavy-rimmed glasses hid the shyness in his hazel eyes. To one side of him was his heavily pregnant sister and her husband. Gray's right arm circled the waist of Pammie, a pretty, twenty-five year old American PhD student who, that night, would promise to marry him but who would be snatched from his grasp two years later by a former high school boyfriend when she returned to Philadelphia to make arrangements for her permanent return to the UK.

Returning to *Initiate*, the scene had shifted. Two heavily tattooed men wearing vests and jogging bottoms were standing in a bleak room. At the bay window hung dirty curtains with a faded, indistinct pattern. Mattresses and cushions shared the floor space with a grubby formica-topped table.

A wide-screened TV was mounted on the wall. One of the men, a thin, unshaven individual with a hawk tattooed on the back of his head, was fiddling at the mountings with a screwdriver. He wheeled round angrily to the other who was holding a phone.

"Fuck sake Daz. Eleven?!"

"It wasn't my idea, Hawkie. Annie just said she's coming. But there's eleven-year-olds and eleven-year-olds, mate. Why don't we wait and see? We can always give her a can of coke and send her home."

"Too late then, isn't it. At that age they blab. Fucking eleven!"

As Daz laid out the potential advantages of bringing the girl into their midst, Hawkie jabbed his screwdriver at the TV mountings in a manner that threatened imminent loss of self-control. Gracia had once told Gray that the actor who played Hawkie was a lovely, gentle person who, since he had been a little boy, had cared for a tortoise named Jane.

Gray had asked, "What about the other actresses? Are they nice?"

She had riled in response. "Actresses? That's so sexist. We're actors. Female barristers don't get called barristresses or anything else different, do they?"

Fair point, but he had never heard a waitress complain.

"Are they nice?"

"So so. They're all right."

Gray did not press her. He knew he was hardly likely to elicit news of a close female friendship since Gracia had never surrounded herself with girlfriends. In any event, it was unusual for her to share with him even a small amount of detail about her life. Their relationship since day one had been bewilderingly difficult. He realised that his mind was wandering away from the increasingly distasteful conversation that was playing out in *Initiate*, clicked PAUSE and went for a pee.

Outwardly, Gracia's behaviour had been rude, uncompromising, often aggressive. He was advised by a string of counsellors and pastoral tutors at her boarding school that inwardly she was angry; angry with her parents for abandoning her, angry with her friends for having proper families, angry with anyone who mispronounced her name. "For God's sake. It rhymes with lacier and racier, get it?" she would snap at anyone who hazarded a guess. She was angry with her school for keeping her on and being so fucking understanding all the time despite every effort she made to get expelled. Most of all she was angry with Gray for not being someone else: mother, father, loving grandparents, a friend even, as all others fell beside the wayside of her alienating behaviour. On one unforgettable Sunday when he had arranged to take her out with the family of another girl who had appeared to show the promise of friendship, Gracia had spat at him outside the school chapel and then sat in silence throughout lunch. The other girl had looked sorrowful and helpless as Gracia blocked her every attempt at camaraderie. The girl's mother had asked in a hushed voice if he ever wondered if he was over-compensating for the loss of Gracia's parents. Was she not, at the end of the day, just a bit spoilt?

During the holidays, their home was a battlefield. Au pairs were engaged for the first few years. Gray grew accustomed to greeting young and enthusiastic Europeans whose principal objective for being there was to improve their English, then shaking hands at the end of the holidays, knowing that his would be the last household in the world that they would wish to return to.

Gracia had rebelled and drawn attention to herself. She had dyed her hair, then shaved her head, worn black, played music to upset the neighbours, sworn, given up eating, announced that she was gay, then that she was not, ignored the au pairs and railed and screamed at Gray for being useless and just the fucking twat who stopped her having fun.

Returning to the snug, Gray unpaused *Initiate*. The altercation between the two paedophiles was interrupted by the appearance of Annie at the door. She sauntered in.

"Four! Not bad for a day's work?"

Hawkie rounded on her. *"Fucking eleven-year-olds is it now, Annie? Eleven! This isn't a fucking creche. What were you thinking? The more commission the merrier? We want quality not quantity. Did you forget that?"*

Annie stood her ground. *"It wasn't like that. If she couldn't come, the other two wouldn't. Neeugh! She can watch TV. I'll make sure she doesn't come back."*

The man stepped closer to her, holding the screwdriver level with the zip of her jeans. *"You'd better, Annie."* It was a disturbing scene.

Through Gracia's teenage years, Gray had had no idea how to cope. He tried friendship. She mocked his attempts. He tried discipline, imposed curfews, banned smoking and excessive drinking. The merest suggestion of soft drugs would be a matter for the police. He let her be in no doubt about that. She found ways to sidestep every limitation including getting a friend she had made in Battersea Park to stab her in the nose and insert a stud into the bloodied hole. In exhaustion, he resorted to simply loving her, unconditionally and without limit. To Gray, his niece was a lost orphan who had a score to settle with life. To love her was all that he could do.

Gracia was bright but put all her effort into underachieving. When she was sixteen she scraped just enough GCSE's to qualify her to enrol on a drama course at the local college and demanded to be allowed to leave both school and home and rent a room on her own. Before that she had never expressed any interest in acting. Come to that, she had never expressed any interest in anything. She was financially secure as a result of her parents' death and had not lived with Gray since the day she slammed the van door shut and did not wave goodbye. Nor had anyone else. And yet he loved her.

The scene in *Initiate* had been interrupted by the arrival of a social worker. There was a fleeting glimpse of Annie running upstairs to an attic space where sat a group of poorly dressed young girls.

"One squeak out of any of you and you're done. Get it?" she threatened in a whisper.

WHAT LIES BENEATH THE SURFACE

Gray recognised both the tone of voice and facial expression that no one in their right mind would argue with. Ruefully, he felt glad that they were now being put to positive use.

He had faithfully observed Christmas and every birthday and ensured that she knew she was always welcome. Gracia came and went as she pleased.

Occasionally she would turn up with a bag and announce that she was staying for a couple of days and then live as if his house were her home. Alternatively, gaps of two or three months might pass during which Gray would hear nothing from her at all. Four years ago, during one of these periods, she had married an Italian travel journalist named Claudio Benettini. The marriage had struck Gray as being another act of rebellion, carried out merely for the triumph of being announced to him after the event.

"I've met someone. Actually, we got married a fortnight ago." Gracia was standing in the kitchen watching him cook omelettes for a Saturday lunch.

That was it.

"Oh?" Gray was accustomed to disappointment where Gracia was concerned. He was not particularly romantic, but he had imagined that there might come a day when he would accompany her down an aisle somewhere. He had never succeeded in forming a mental image of the groom.

"You could meet him if you like," she offered.

"That would be nice. I'd like to. Have you known each other long?"

"Long enough."

"Only you've not mentioned him before."

"Well, I have now. He's Italian."

"Oh. Right. How nice. Where are you going to live?"

"Where I live now. Claudio travels a lot. He's got an apartment in Perugia so we'll spend time there too, obviously."

And it was arranged that she and Claudio would come for lunch the next day.

Gray cooked lamb. "Bit of a cliché, meat and two veg," he fretted to himself when it was too late to prepare anything different. He need not have worried. The menu was a fraction of the cliché embodied by Claudio.

He was of short stature, neatly dressed in jacket and chinos over brown leather shoes. A scarf hung loosely around his neck. Dark curls jostled for space at collar length. His well-defined cheek bones sat beneath shining lustrous, lustful brown eyes which rarely moved from Gracia. He greeted Gray formally and complimented him on the location of his apartment, its decor, his cuisine and his niece, on whose thigh he rested his left hand whenever he raised his glass to his lips.

Gracia sat beside him with the air of a trophy winner. She lauded Claudio's writing, his heritage and the one thing that Gray had never been able to provide, his family, all of whom had attended the wedding in a village beside one of the Italian lakes. Gracia said she had considered inviting Gray but had decided against it because she had known that he would be too busy.

Gray gleaned that the couple had first met by chance at an event at the National Portrait Gallery. They had known each other for precisely four months.

"For God's sake, no, Gray, I'm not pregnant," retaliated Gracia as they stacked the plates in the kitchen while Claudio sipped wine and regarded the view across the Square from the sitting room. She was responding to the careful enquiry Gray had risked in order to find some explanation for what had already struck him as an early decision to marry. "God, you are so cynical. We just knew it was right. Why wait?"

Gray could think of several reasons; seeing how things panned out once the initial urgency of physical contact had calmed down a little being just one of them, but he did not say.

Over the following years he gained the impression that the couple rarely met but he knew that Gracia would never admit to him that she had made a mistake. If she talked about her husband's prolonged absences at all, it would be to roll her eyes as she slowly and pointedly explained the simple need for him to tour abroad in order to see the places he wrote about. Gray hoped that she knew that if the marriage failed, he was the one person on whom she would be able to rely. To him this was an unquestionable truth, but he never found the right moment to tell her. If he had done, he suspected she would only have shrugged.

From the little she shared with him, it was clear to Gray that *Initiate* was potentially career-changing. For ten years after completing her drama course, Gracia had worked in bars and restaurants, or touted for charities on the street in between small, poorly paid acting jobs. Her casting in *Initiate* had come about through an agent who had watched her agonised and haunting portrayal of an abused holocaust victim in a play at an Islington pub theatre.

REGENT'S CANAL BRIDGE NO. 9

EARLY EVENING

A turbaned head leant over Davey. Large brown eyes gazed at him with loathing. The face was young. No amount of sustained hatred brought about by an indoctrinated and zealous belief in religious right, no amount of fighting in defence of territory can disguise the softness of adolescent lips nor newly sprouted stubble.

"Get up! It's your time." The voice was also unmistakably youthful.

They were in a windowless concrete cell. Davey had been lying on the ground, sleeping. The soldier jabbed a gun into his back. He stood up and tried to take a step forward. Chains around his ankles restrained him and he fell back down to the ground. The youth laughed. Others, hitherto unnoticed by Davey, joined in.

Two of them pulled him across the earthen floor towards a door as the soldier continued to jab him in the back. When the door opened, light flooded into the cell. They stepped out into searing heat. Concrete walls surrounded them. He was prodded and dragged to a wall opposite the door. An oval shaped red mark stained the centre. Davey was propped against it by his wingmen. He stood awkwardly, bent sideways, wavering involuntarily. "Stand up!" screamed the turbaned youth. "Get back!" he ordered generally.

Davey looked down the barrel of the gun pointed at him. An explosion rang through his head. He opened his eyes, expecting the glare of hot sun, pain, and a further blast. Silence. No pain. The light was grey and dull. He looked around warily for his jailers. No jailers. The concrete compound had disappeared and all he could see on either side of him was vegetation, the structure of a bridge and water.

"Jesus Christ!" he said. And he drew his knees up to his chest and slowly sank back into sleep, thanking God that he was alive.

TOP FLOOR FLAT, NORTH GATE MANSION BLOCK, ST JOHN'S WOOD
6:05pm

She was late. Nothing new about that. Unpredictability had always been part of Gracia's appeal but Patrick couldn't remember the last time he'd felt so apprehensive.

He had not been looking for extra-marital pleasure. He loved his wife, after all and their married life was what lawyers euphemistically described as full, meaning they still had regular, pleasant enough sex. But the necessity of spending the working week away from home lent itself to unfamiliar solitude. Colleagues who found themselves similarly placed had discovered that the opera and theatre filled the free time spent away from their wives and for the first year or so of living in London he had followed their example. Gracia had entered his life as an unexpected guest, but one whose presence caused all other diversions to dull by comparison. Her perspective on life roller-coastered between extremes and never paused between. And my God, he enjoyed the ride.

Occasionally her mood was reflected in her choice of clothes. Printed clowns threw playful shapes around her favourite blouse, a sultry panther hung languidly around the shoulder of another, snakeskin constricted skin-tight leggings. Post-shower freshness was perfectly represented in a kimono decorated with orange blossom and roses. Birds and butterflies expressed liberation. The kings and queens of the jungle spoke danger, monkeys fun. Block colours made her feel boring, she once told him. Stripes gave her height and a feeling of control. She never wore check. She was five foot four inches tall and they made her feel small and cross, she said. One day she turned up in a long-sleeved, elephant-print maxi dress.

"What's this about then?" he had asked, wondering whether the elephants were a subtle pointer to the fact that she had remembered something clever or some other characteristic of elephants that he could not now recall.

"I'm fat, I've put on weight." she had replied. At eight stone it was hard to make herself look as enormous as she said she felt but she blew out her cheeks and looked down at herself, crossly.

"Let's see." He lifted her into his arms. "Mmm." He laughed as he landed a kiss on her nose. "I'm not sure I'd go so far as to say fat but I could help you burn off a few calories before dinner, if you want."

Her handling of money lurched between irresponsible extravagance and unrealistic parsimony. She would offer to cook and he would arrive home, tired after a day of verbal conflict, never knowing whether to expect spaghetti or caviar. She could laugh or cry herself helpless at box sets, but if the series failed to engage her she would abandon it with a petulant click of the remote control and ask what they could do now. And what they would do now was make unrestrained and wildly enjoyable love. She would arch, grab and cry out, despatching who knew what demons in her moment of release.

For two years, he had enjoyed a passion that far outran the conventional love-making that had become established at home. But how she could rage! On the phone she would berate complete strangers whose service had failed to reach the impossibly high standards she expected. Then, exasperated and spent, she would turn to him for a reaction. He would raise an eyebrow and she would laugh, toss her head and appear to forget all about it. And he would laugh along, with no feeling for her victim or how her fury might affect that person's day.

Tonight though, he himself faced the prospect of being the object of her anger and there was no-one there to break the mood. He tried to create a version of the story that blamed Gray for the whole cock-up on account of being the person they hadn't been able to let in on the secret of their affair. But who was he trying to kid?

He re-read the message that he had sent to Gray that afternoon and cringed.

How could he have been so careless? Gracia Peel was listed immediately above Graham Andrew in his list of contacts. That was how. He had been aware of the fact and always taken care to double check his addressee before clicking Send. Today he had been so thrilled with the content of his message he had forgotten to check who would receive it.

He considered pouring himself another drink. No, better wait. Picked the cucumber from his glass, threw it in the bin and put the glass beside the sink. Looked around. Washed the glass. Waited. Dried the glass and replaced it in the cupboard. Then the buzzer sounded.

Gracia's arrival was explosive. The front door handle slammed into the wall beside it as she entered, a whirlwind of blue and indigo cotton wrapped around hostility in the guise of unblemished beauty beneath a wig whose blackness perfectly depicted her mood. Patrick also noticed the tiger print.

"You fucking twat! How fucking embarrassing do you think this is?"

Don't rise to it, he told himself. Apologise, apologise, apologise.

"Darling I'm so sorry. I'm an idiot. I know."

One apology was never enough.

"You might as well have sent a picture of your fucking dick."

"I know, I'm so sorry."

Gracia pulled off her wig. Her blonde hair tumbled onto her shoulders.

He longed to stroke it but was kept at a distance by a further battery.

"Gray, of all people! He's as good as my fucking Dad. How many times have I said that Gray mustn't find out about us? Which bit of your tiny brain didn't catch on?"

He didn't like that.

"I've said I'm sorry, Gracia. What more do you want me to say?"

By now she was in the sitting room, standing with her back to the bookcase. Even this wrong-footed him. She usually went straight to the kitchen or bedroom. She looked at him, her eyes bright and woundingly hard.

"You can't say anything, can you? I'm the one who's going to have to look him in the eye again, thanks to you. What the fuck am I supposed to tell him? Sorry, Gray, I've been shagging your best mate for two years, didn't I mention that?"

Patrick decided it might help to try to reason. "He's a man of the world."

It did not.

"Oh, what, you're saying that Gray does shit like this too? I don't think so. He's a man with some principles, which is more than can be said of you."

He knew Gracia was a fighter. Maybe he should change tack, go on the offensive.

"Or you."

"I'm sorry?"

The look in her eye told him to backtrack fast. "Nothing. Sorry."

"No. Please explain, Patrick?"

"I'm just saying that when it comes to lofty principles, I don't think either of us is in a position to boast."

"Well, thank you for pointing that out. You certainly know how to make an apology."

Sarcasm did not become her. Patrick felt the whole argument was in danger of descending to mud-slinging. He hit on an idea to stop it now.

"Darling. Shush. Come to bed. We can make this okay."

For a microsecond, he wondered if she was thinking about it.

"You are joking?"

Patrick began to feel annoyed. He did not like to be mocked. She had had her tantrum. Surely it was time to start talking rationally.

"Come on Gracia. It was a stupid mistake. Gray was always going to find out one day. He'll get over it."

"Oh you think so, do you? Jesus Christ, Patrick. This isn't about Gray. We are talking about me here."

"Silly of me. Of course we are."

He deeply regretted those words.

"Oh, fuck off."

"Why not have a drink? It'll calm you down."

"Calm me down? Is that all that's wrong? You really have no idea, do you. I'm going."

She picked up her bag.

"Oh, come on Gracia. Don't overreact." God, he wished he hadn't said that.

"Don't you fucking dare tell me not to overreact. You've not only embarrassed me but this is about trust, Patrick. How do I know you're not going to do something like this again? I know you're sick and tired of me talking about *Initiate*." (He had never said that.) "But finally, finally, I'm getting some recognition and I am just not willing to risk you fucking the whole thing up again by twatting around on your phone and sending messages intended for me to God knows who else."

"It's hardly likely to happen again, Gracia."

"But I don't know that, do I? Next time it could be Jenny and she might forward it to a tabloid or something."

He didn't like Jenny being brought into the conversation. Gracia was now being ridiculous and he spoke unkindly.

"People aren't that interested in you, Gracia."

"Thanks for that. Appreciated. Funny though because I thought over a million followers on Instagram showed that they were interested."

She started pacing back and forth in front of the window. They were on the fourth floor. Behind her he could see the green expanse of Regent's Park. He would have loved to have been there now but on she ranted.

"You don't have a clue, do you? Let me spell it out. The producers of *Initiate* will like me for as long as I am good for their brand. That's not going to be the case if it gets out that I'm sleazing around with another man. I'm married too, in case you've forgotten."

Patrick considered this.

"Well, if we're talking celebrity gossip, I'd have thought that's exactly what the producers would want."

"Which only goes to prove how little you know."

"Anyway, Jenny wouldn't forward anything to the tabloids. She's not like that."

"I would if I were your wife."

"But you're not, are you."

Shouldn't have said that. Definitely shouldn't have said that.

"No I'm not. But the good thing is – thank fuck. And I don't just mean because of this shit storm you've created. Christ! Claudio may not be the answer to all my hopes and dreams but at least he knows his way around a fucking keyboard."

He could not think of a single thing to say.

She stopped pacing and turned to him. Her look had changed from anger to acceptance.

"I'm sorry Patrick. Well, no, I'm not sorry actually, but to be honest there's too much at stake for me now. Can we just call this a day because I think we're done here, don't you? Don't argue with me. I really don't have the energy."

Without waiting for a reply, she walked through to the bedroom. His spirits rose. Gracia was the only person in the world he could imagine making a decision that was so utterly inconsistent with what she had just said.

"Are we ...?"

"Oh my God. You actually think – I can't believe you. I'm getting my stuff."

Now he was utterly at sea.

"Gracia, don't."

"Fine. I'll just go then."

He felt he had no choice but to let her do whatever she wanted. "I'll call you an Uber."

"Christ. You could at least look as if you mind about this. No thank you. I'd rather walk."

"Don't take the canal path."

"I'll be fine."

"If you're going that way I'm not letting you go on your own."

"Do what you like, Patrick."

She replaced the wig and walked to the front door. Over her shoulder she snapped, "Are you coming or not?"

MANCHESTER SQUARE, MARYLEBONE

MID EVENING

Hawkie was leaning against a cupboard in a grubby kitchenette watching a young girl stir a dented pan which rocked unsteadily on top of a filthy stove. She was barefoot, wearing shorts and a sleeveless top. The carpet burn at the top of her spine spoke more than Gray cared to imagine. The plot of the drama was not obscure, but his mind had wandered throughout too much of the current episode and he was going to have to start it again. He decided to make supper instead and, as he moved through to the kitchen, his mind took him unwillingly back to thinking about Patrick and Gracia.

It was a revelation that they were intimate, no doubt about that. He had to think carefully what it was that bothered him about the relationship. He was no prude. People had affairs the whole time. And it wasn't hard to work out what they saw in each other. Patrick was attractive and charming. Twenty years older than Gracia. A father figure? Was that another fuck off to Gray? Gracia's appeal was obvious. Still young but no longer naive, a beauty with crystal blue eyes and an indomitable, free-wheeling spirit. Even so, Gray could not help but feel that the relationship between Patrick and Gracia would bring chaos and sadness into their lives. He wished such things upon neither of them. He wished too that he had never introduced them to each other.

For a minute or two, hunger took his mind back to the present. He microwaved a meal of fish in sauce with rice that he had picked up at a decent frozen food shop. As he ate, his mind went back two years to the party he had given to jointly celebrate his appointment to the High Court Bench and his sixtieth birthday.

Gracia had forced him to organise some kind of gathering. She'd said it would be pathetic not to. The battle of where and how to celebrate had resulted in a truce. Drinks and tapas for thirty in the private room of a Soho bar from 7:30pm. Gray expected most of the guests to leave by 10pm.

Gracia aimed to ensure that it went on till midnight but she was no longer present when the last guest left at 11:30pm. She and Patrick had departed together half an hour earlier. Neither of them had said goodbye, but Gray had been surrounded by friends and neither noticed nor considered the fact, not until now. Was that the beginning of it? How could the thought have never crossed his mind?

Patrick's name had topped the guest list.

"Who's this?" Gracia had been writing the invitations in the kitchen. She tapped his name with her biro.

Gray was seated opposite her. Somehow the process of selecting party guests had turned into an inquisition.

"A barrister. I must have mentioned him. He's a very good friend." Gracia scrunched her nose.

"Hasn't he got a wife?"

"He has but she lives in the country. I doubt if she'll come. But no, you're right, put Mr and Mrs Patrick Kingdom."

"How come he's so important?"

"He isn't so important. He's just a good friend."

"Fine. I'm sure he'll have a great time. Don't you have any friends who aren't lawyers?"

The fact was, he barely did. But Gray had not been wholly honest. Patrick was actually very important to him. It was just that Gray didn't feel inclined to tell Gracia why.

HARROW CROWN COURT

FRIDAY 17TH MAY 2010 4:30pm

Half-way through his first stint sitting as a part-time judge in the Crown Court, Gray was way outside his comfort zone.

His own practice at the Bar was in commercial law. Business, banking, trade – he understood these worlds and was thoroughly acquainted with the rules of law, practice and procedure that governed commercial litigation. For thirty years, as a civil practitioner, he had conducted what was termed a largely paper practice, meaning he rarely attended court and never addressed a jury. It suited him well. Gray was not a natural performer. A tactician, on the other hand, yes. His preference for manoeuvres which were carefully considered, played with deliberation and set out clearly in writing suited him to his work. But in the Crown Court, where the work is all crime, the rules and pace are different, and Gray had no reason to be familiar with them. And yet, as a part-time judge, a recorder, with his first foot on the judicial ladder, he was required to spend three weeks a year presiding in this unfamiliar environment.

When a matter of law or practice arises in court it is the responsibility of the barristers in the case to remind the judge of what he is deemed to know already. In Gray's case, these might be aspects of law with which he was unfamiliar and he relied on counsel to play it straight. But, as in every field, some in the profession are sharp. Winning a case is their sole aim. Assisting the judge with advice which may be contrary to their interest is not their first priority. Other barristers are generous, trustworthy and helpful. It was not always easy to distinguish one from another.

A defendant, Jon Kane, was on trial for burglary. The alleged facts were that he had entered a large suburban house through a downstairs window in the middle of the night and broken into the safe from which he had taken a large sum of cash in US dollars. He was a twenty-six-year-old and had several previous convictions for burglary and two for rape. In evidence, he stated that he would not know how to force open a house safe.

Patrick, as prosecuting counsel, applied to Gray to call rebuttal evidence that one of the defendant's previous convictions was for a burglary in which exactly the same type of safe had been forced open. Defence counsel objected on the basis that Mr Kane claimed he had acted merely as look-out in the earlier case while his co-accused forced the safe, and thus the rebuttal evidence that Patrick applied for Gray's permission to call was irrelevant.

Gray had to decide whether or not to let Patrick put that earlier conviction

WHAT LIES BENEATH THE SURFACE

before the jury. He was unacquainted with both Patrick and defence counsel. They each made their submissions and Gray had absolutely no idea what to do. He adjourned for ten minutes in the hope of asking advice from another judge in the building. But it was a Friday afternoon. The other courts had finished for the day and all the judges had gone home.

Alone in his private room away from the courtroom, he turned the pages of Archbold, the criminal practitioner's bible, a volume that is a good four inches thick. He didn't know where to look. One thing he did know was that if he allowed Patrick to call the evidence and that turned out to be the wrong decision it would provide strong grounds for appeal if the defendant was convicted. A successful appeal against a wrong decision would do his hopes of advancement to a full-time job on the judicial bench no good at all. On the other hand, if he didn't allow the evidence of the previous conviction to be put before the jury, the defendant might be acquitted and thus free to burgle or rape afresh, if so inclined.

Fifteen minutes passed.

Two taps on the door announced the arrival of the court usher who stood at a polite distance, hands neatly folded in front of him over his gown.

"Counsel would like to address you in the absence of the jury, Judge."

Gray returned to court and after the customary bow to Patrick and his opponent he sat down. He raised his eyes. Patrick was on his feet.

"Mr Kingdom?"

"Your Honour. During the adjournment I have had time to consider my application. It raises a matter of law which I now recall is currently the subject of an appeal pending in the Criminal Division. The appellant's name is Holroyde. That being the case, Your Honour, I feel it is only fair to withdraw my application and not seek to call evidence of the previous safe-breaking conviction, if I may put it that way. I have discussed this with defence counsel. We have agreed that if Your Honour would simply not refer in your summing up to the defendant's evidence that he has no idea how to break open that kind of safe then the matter can be left at that and the rebuttal evidence will not be called."

Gray could not have been more relieved. The case proceeded. Patrick made an exemplary closing speech and the defendant went down for two years.

A couple of days later, Gray happened to meet Patrick outside the entrance to the Temple on the Strand. It was early evening. Gray was on his way home, Patrick to El Vino's.

Gray smiled. "Mr Kingdom, hello. I must thank you again for your assistance in the trial at Harrow."

Patrick smiled back."Not at all, Judge. My pleasure. It is strange how these things sometimes work out."

Gray was puzzled. "What do you mean?"

"Well Judge, the funny thing is that when I got back to Chambers that evening I looked again at the case I referred to, Holroyde? The one I mentioned was waiting for a hearing date in the Court of Appeal?

"Oh yes?"

"I'm sorry to say, Judge, I got my wires crossed. The substantive ground of appeal in Holroyde is on a quite different point of law, nothing to do with the issue that arose in Harrow at all, I am afraid."

Gray was far from stupid. He appreciated that Patrick was telling him that he had recognised in Harrow that Gray hadn't known what to do and so had taken the decision away from him. He raised his eyebrows.

"Really Mr Kingdom?"

"But not to worry, Judge. We potted Mr Kane. That was the main thing. He's a nasty piece of work, more likely to rape than burgle. Unfortunately, this burglary was all the police had on him."

Gray looked at him steadily with a hint of a smile. "Well Mr Kingdom. I'm more grateful than I realised."

"Don't mention it, Judge. Glad to help."

"How about we call into El Vino's? I think that would be appropriate."

"Nothing I'd like more."

They were able to find a relatively quiet corner away from the boisterous gossip and banter of early evening drinkers. Gray bought a bottle of red, which they drank as they agreed on first name terms and chatted.

Gray brought up the Harrow trial again.

"You took a hell of a risk, didn't you? Evidence of Kane's previous conviction for a similar offence would have got the conviction home and dry. Why let it go?"

"I have no idea really," laughed Patrick. "I hope it doesn't become a habit." He thought for a moment. "Actually, I do know."

"And?"

"At the time I really wasn't sure of the law, but I was absolutely sure that I didn't want there to be a successful appeal against you if it had turned out that you had made the wrong decision."

"Why ever not? We've never met."

"I know. But one gets to recognise class acts on the Bench in this game."

"So, you did it to save my bacon?"

"Not only that."

"Oh?"

Patrick raised his glass and sat back.

"I felt the jury were with me and wanted to keep the advantage. I couldn't have borne to see my opponent win, not even on appeal. He was a shifty git. Pissed me off all week."

As Patrick took a mouthful of wine, Gray sat back also. Such generosity was rare.

"Well thank you, Patrick."

Patrick swallowed appreciatively. "Please, don't mention it."

And they were friends.

Whenever they were both in London they would meet for dinner and exchange stories of the unpredictable behaviour of litigants they had encountered and sometimes, "strictly entre nous" as they would say, their solicitors, barristers and judges. Some years later, Gray had been delighted to advise Patrick throughout the process of applying for silk and, by then well on the way to the High Court Bench himself, had been Patrick's referee. When Patrick's application was successful Gray had attended a celebratory drinks party in Chambers and been introduced to Jenny and the boys as the man without whom it couldn't have happened.

REGENT'S CANAL. BRIDGE NO. 8 TO PRIMROSE HILL BRIDGE

7:05pm

The evening light was grey and limpid. Heavy cloud obstructed any warmth from the sun. Patrick had pressed for them to walk along Prince Albert Road to Primrose Hill, but, in order to be as difficult as possible, Gracia had insisted that they drop down to the canal path which ran parallel to Prince Albert Road. It was a quiet route that they'd often taken together. Banks of trees and ill-kept shrubbery lined both sides of the canal, concealing it from the traffic on the main road to the north and from Regent's Park to the south. By day the path was popular with walkers, cyclists and joggers. As darkness fell, the fitness-conscious gave ground to drinkers, addicts, dealers and others bent on ruining rather than improving physical health, who were able to deal, drink and score out of sight of the public gaze. This evening there were fewer runners and walkers than Gracia had expected. It annoyed her to be glad of Patrick's company. Fresh air had cooled the heat of boiling rage within her. She was annoyed with him, for sure, but, she asked herself, did she really want to call the whole thing off? One more apology and she might weaken. It was up to him now.

"Would you like me to talk to Gray?" he asked.

A chivalrous offer, but he was going to have to try harder than that.

"What's the point? He knows all he needs to now, doesn't he?"

"It might help him to know that we were serious about each other?"

Gracia noticed his use of the past tense and replied defensively.

"Really?"

They walked on in silence. A young man, cropped hair flattened by headphones, wearing a vest and shorts ran past them, head down, feet beating a regular rhythm, locked into his own world of self-motivation and fitness. Patrick carried on speaking.

"I never thought this was just an affair you know, Gracia. I really thought we might be something together one day."

"Did you?"

"You didn't?"

She considered this and spoke truthfully.

"I've been, I don't know what, serious, I suppose. But long term? Come on. You'd never have thrown everything up for me."

She would have liked a denial. He repeated his offer. "I'll talk to Gray."

"And say what?"

"Tell him we loved each other?"

She noticed the rising inflection. Was he telling her that he'd loved her or merely enquiring whether that would be a good line to spin to Gray? And the past tense. 'Loved', not 'love'. That small 'd' told her that he had accepted that the relationship was over and wasn't willing to argue for it. Fine. All he seemed to be doing now was attempting to create a frictionless, tidy ending with no loose ends to nag at him in future. Resentment settled itself into the vacuum that her earlier anger had vacated.

She replied sulkily, "Don't know what difference that'll make but go ahead if you want. I'm not going to. It's his fault anyway. He introduced us."

She didn't see the 'that's not really fair' face Patrick pulled. He made a joke.

"Are you really as miserable as you look, or just making a special effort for tonight?"

The first words he had ever spoken to her.

She had been standing in the corner of the room at Gray's party wearing a white silk blouse and culottes, watching middle-aged men in suits with mumsie wives quaff and chat about nothing that interested her. She had observed Patrick arrive, alone, and had watched him as he leant towards Gray. She overheard "Tummy bug. Sends her apologies," then noticed his eyes sweep the room, resting on her for a fraction of a second before he was greeted with bonhomie by one of the suited men. Thirty minutes later he strolled over. She had never forgiven him for those thirty minutes during which somebody's wife had approached her and shrieked, "Hello. Who are you here with?"

Gracia looked around the room. To be fair, she was apparently the only unaccompanied woman in the assembly of well-heeled, well-fed couples. She bit back the 'aren't I allowed to be here on my own?' repost and replied, "Nobody. My husband works abroad."

"Oh, how exciting! What does he do?"

And stimulated by Gracia's reply, the woman had enthused about the romantic Italian husband she could picture, his fascinating job, the holidays she had enjoyed with her husband beside Lake Como. She had not asked what Gracia herself did and had eventually blended back into the body of the gathering in quest of her other half and a top up.

Patrick had appeared beside her and his eyes had twinkled as he launched his opening gambit. She could not help herself and had laughed. The words had rarely failed to make her smile whenever he had repeated them since, but this time they fell flat. She wasn't in the mood for playful reminiscences and didn't respond.

A young couple walked past them from the other direction, chatting. Gracia caught a fragment. "And Phil, that's Ryan's boyfriend, he turned round and said…", Gracia would never know what Phil had said. Briefly she envied their simple happiness. This was shit and not what she wanted.

Anticipating the awkward goodbye that would have to take place sooner or later she just wanted it over with.

"Listen, I'm going to go on alone now."

She turned to him. Patrick was smiling. She followed his look towards a man jogging towards them. Clean shaven, fit, early forties. Pleasant face. He slowed down and smiled in greeting.

"Evening Patrick." The man had an upper-class accent, not dissimilar from Patrick's own. Inwardly, Gracia prayed they would not have to chat.

"James." Patrick slowed his pace.

James looked at Gracia. She dreaded seeing the familiar look of recognition that lit up strangers' eyes when they met her. The wig would do its job of hiding her hair but damn the decision not to wear sunglasses. Was he the type to watch *Initiate*? Lost in that moment of thought she caught the tip of her boot on an uneven brick in the path and tripped into a puddle.

"Neeugh!"

Patrick took her arm. "All right?"

"Yeah I'm fine." She looked down at his hand on her arm.

James said, "I'll go on. See you Patrick." He inclined his head to Gracia and continued on his way.

"Who was that?" she asked.

"James Mitchell, one of the chaps in Chambers. I've seen him along here before. I think he lives nearby."

It was cold. They walked beneath the span of a large brick bridge supported by solid rotund, ribbed iron columns. At the top of the slopes beneath the arches on either side of the canal lay shady, silent, disquieting signs of life cocooned in sleeping bags and cardboard. She knew it was only five minutes or so's walk to the next bridge which was where she would leave the canal to cross to Primrose Hill. She wanted to be alone.

They walked on for a minute or so. To their left, the messy undergrowth was temporally relieved by a heavily graffitied brick wall topped with wire netting. She stopped.

"Look we're nearly there, I can go on my own from here."

"Oh." He sounded surprised. "Are you sure?'

He did not insist on staying with her.

"Sure."

"Gracia." He stopped and gently took hold of her upper arm to turn her towards him. "One last kiss, please?"

She didn't reply.

"Take off the wig, Gracia. Be you."

It wasn't worth arguing. She dragged the wig from her head. He pushed his fingers through her hair. She lifted her mouth towards his.

REGENT'S CANAL – BRIDGE NO. 9

6:50pm

Since the nightmare, Davey had slept more soundly and now he felt rested. Despite the warmth of his sleeping bag, he felt the penetrating cold of a strong and hard support against his back. His stubble snagged on nylon as he raised his head from his bag to look around. Behind him was the stone abutment of the bridge. Above him was the first of three brick arches which spanned the canal. At the foot of the concrete slope in front of him was a footpath from which rose five tall ribbed iron pillars matched by five on the other side of the still, silent waterway. Between them, these monoliths supported the massive centre arch. Opposite him a slope led up to the abutment on the other side of the canal.

He looked around for signs of life. All was quiet. Any other nocturnal visitors who might arrive had yet to appear, one in particular. Sometimes when he awoke she would be sitting silently beside him. She always let him sleep. He craned his neck from side to side. No, he was alone.

He needed a piss. He pushed the bag down to his legs, eased them out and scrambled across the slope on all fours. His face and head itched and he swept his hands and knuckles over his forehead and around his cheeks to the back of his head, wiping his crusted eyes and ears with his fingertips. To his left was an unkempt bank of undergrowth. He stumbled and slid to a tree and stood with one hand leaning against the time-scored bark. Relief was welcome, but he was starving and thirsty.

He returned to his bag and rummaged around for food or water. Six inches of cider slopped around in a bottle. He necked it and tossed the empty container aside. Starving. He felt the pockets of his trousers "No. No." Tried his bag again. A chocolate bar. Saliva moistened the inside of his mouth. "No, that was for her, a present. There must be something else. Nothing. What? Yes! Sausage roll. You beauty." He pushed two inches into his mouth and started chewing as he felt around for what else he might find. A little package slid between his fingers. "Lucky or what? You darling girl. You love me. I love you." He took tobacco, papers and lighter from the side pocket of his bag and flicked out a Rizla. With a deftness acquired over two decades of practice he spread the tobacco, sprinkled spice, rolled, licked and rolled the paper again then put the spliff into his mouth. "Light. Fuck sake. Light." He inhaled. Better than sex. He breathed in, swallowed and waited for the feeling to engulf his brain. Then he gave himself up. "Love. I love you. Beautiful, beautiful world."

Two young men walked by along the path below him. One looked up to the top of the concrete slope. Davey nodded. The young man did not. He took a few more drags. Here was a bloke running. Smile at him, call hello. "Hello." Nothing. Fucker. He wanted Rosie. "I'll walk to meet her. Yeah." He looked left and then right, disoriented. Thoughts jostled for space in his mind as a couple passed from right to left in front of him. His eyes followed them then narrowed with the effort of making a logical decision. "She'll be coming from that way, the way this bloke and his pretty dark haired girl are going." He slid down the concrete slope and stood up, tried to balance himself squarely on both feet as his eyes lost and then regained focus, then began to walk after them. They had not turned back to look at him. His legs and feet felt distant, unreliable. The couple stopped a little way in front of him. He looked again. The woman had changed. Blonde now. "Jesus, the bloke's got two women on the go!" He took a couple of steps in their direction and looked again. "No, wait, that's Rosie. My Rosie. What's she doing with this bastard? What the fuck? He's touching her hair." He broke into a charge. "You bastard, stop! No! You don't kiss her. Smack your fucking head."

"Leave him." Patrick urged.

She hesitated, "But he might be hurt."

"Come on. Leave him. Quick. Run!"

"We can't just …"

"Gracia, for Christ's sake. Get away from him."

Patrick pulled her to her feet and dragged her away.

"He's fine. Just winded. He's high. Drunk. You can smell it. He'll be fine. Come on! Before he gets up!"

They ran to the base of the slope leading to Primrose Hill Bridge. Regent's Park lay to their right, Prince Albert Road to their left, with Primrose Hill beyond. Patrick stopped and stood with his hands on his hips, breathing heavily.

He looked back towards the path. "Come on."

Gracia clumsily replaced her wig as she followed him up the slope.

Patrick stopped beside the zebra crossing on Prince Albert Road and rubbed his side. "Jesus!"

"Are you okay?" she asked in concern.

He nodded. "I'm okay." Then he touched the side of his head. Pain cried out from a developing bruise. He looked at his fingers. No blood. He took a moment, then asked her.

"Are you?"

"Yes, I'm just shocked. Why did he do that?" she asked.

"Off his head I expect. He didn't try to get my wallet or either of our phones. Just went straight for me. Bastard practically knocked my head off." His hand returned to his head.

"Are you sure you're okay?

"Yes I'm fine. Fuck sake. Come on. I'll take you home." He didn't want to let her go.

"No it's fine. It's only ten minutes. I can go on my own. The path across the Hill is lit. I'll be fine. I'd rather."

He didn't want to push it. "Are you sure."

She nodded.

He looked at her. She hesitated then turned away to cross the road. "Goodbye then, Patrick."

TWO HOURS LATER

"Davey love, you're hurt."

Davey thought he was dreaming. He'd known she'd come. And here she was, crouching down beside him.

"My lovely girl," he said quietly.

"What did you do to your wrist?" She looked frightened to touch it but her fingertips lightly brushed the swollen joint.

"Oh, it's nothing." He tried to hide it but it hurt and her eyes, her beautiful grey eyes, looked sad. Tentatively, she took the wrist in her hand. The pain bore no relation to the gentleness of her touch.

"Shite, that hurts."

She told him he must go to the hospital.

"Don't be soft."

"Can you stand up?"

He could. She held his elbow as he walked gingerly back towards the bridge where he had left his stuff. Together they climbed up the slope.

"I booked the top floor, for the sea view. Only they done us over because it's only a canal." He managed a short laugh.

She asked again, "Davey, what happened?"

He told her he'd been in a bit of a fight.

She ran her hand over his head and said, "That's a nasty bump you've got there. Did he do that to you?"

And Davey winced a little and said, "No, I just fell over. I'm a clumsy eejit, you know that, Rosie."

And then he explained.

"I thought she was you, Rosie. He was kissing a girl and I thought she was you. Her hair was long and fair like yours and I had to stop him so I hit him, Rosie. Then he winded me and I fell on my wrist. It'll mend, don't worry. Kiss me, Rosie."

Her lips were chapped but her tongue was soft. After a minute she stopped and drew back, then looked at him, all serious, and said "Davey, you shouldn't stay round here. He'll go to the police. They'll come."

And he said, "Rosie, you worry too much. We'll have a drink and a smoke. OK? We'll have a little sleep and then I'll go?"

And she smiled and said, "OK."

And they drank and smoked and then they fell asleep.

Gray took his wine glass into the kitchen and put it on the worktop. He was too tired to empty the dishwasher and could not be bothered to wash it up. He turned off the light and went up the stairs to his bedroom. It was always at this time of night that Vanessa came into his mind.

The timing had been all wrong. There had been occasional girlfriends since Pammie but no-one serious between her departure and Gray's family tragedy. Natural shyness and the demands of establishing a successful practice collaborated to inhibit a florid love life. Vanessa had been introduced to him at a Middle Temple Christmas party a year after Gray had moved to Clapham. She was a slim, pleasant faced, family practitioner, a widow with strawberry blonde hair and a gentle look in her eye. Her husband had died of testicular cancer six years previously, so no children.

She had expressed sympathetic interest when Gray described his living arrangement.

"Heavens. I was not expecting you to say that."

"Oh?" He asked. "What were you expecting?" He appreciated the fact that she had not shied away from the subject. In casual chat most of his colleagues kept to safer topics of conversation such as their work or favourite eating establishments rather than close enquiry into his home life.

"I suppose something more predictable. I don't know. Maybe a fireside cat to go home to or something. Not a twelve-year-old girl. How incredibly good of you. Gosh, it can't be easy."

"Not always." Gray could afford to treat the subject lightly. Gracia did not break up for a few days and for now he was enjoying respite. "But even without my niece I think I'd have held on for a few more years before installing the fireside cat. After all, I wouldn't want it to eat my slippers."

And Vanessa had blushed. "Oh God, sorry. I didn't mean that."

"Good," Gray replied. And he had meant it. He did not want this girl to think he was old. Younger than him she may be have been, but there can't have been that many years between them.

It was five in fact. She was thirty-six.

The following day Gray had received a message.

> Dear Gray
> I am having a few people over for drinks on the 21st December.
> Would love you to come. Do bring Gracia.
> Vanessa

And gradually, once more, Gray had fallen love.

Gently, Vanessa had transformed Gray into a more modern version of himself. She was responsible for the advent of contact lenses in place of heavy spectacles.

"There!" she had said triumphantly. "Now we can see your eyes. You look half your age."

"You look wrong," said Gracia. "Like you're crying all the time."

Vanessa had made changes to his wardrobe also, consigning ill-advised cords and brogues to charity shops in favour of well-cut casual trousers and lightweight shoes.

"It's embarrassing," complained Gracia. "None of the other fathers dress like that."

"Other fathers" had been a small gift wrapped in condemnation.

Vanessa sometimes teased Gray about the moustache that he had grown in the post-Pammie era. One day she pointed out lightheartedly that white bristles were taking over. Gray had got so used to the moustache that he had never taken much notice of it but when he looked in the mirror that evening he saw what she meant. The following morning he shaved it off. Gracia had erupted.

"But I liked it. Why does she get to decide how you look all the time?"

Gray had assured her that the decision had been entirely his and nothing to do with Vanessa.

"Yeah, right."

Notwithstanding Vanessa's occasional and, Gray would have thought, unimportant alterations to his life, both adults were aware that Gracia had to be handled sensitively. Their relationship grew strong and close during the school holidays but Vanessa retained her own flat and Gray took care to give priority to what he perceived as Gracia's need for stability and security during the vacations and exeat weekends.

It was not enough.

When Gracia was fourteen they had taken her to Center Parcs. As a holiday it had appeared to offer a varied enough programme of activities and potential for friendship-making to entertain Gracia, who, at that time, quite enjoyed sport. Gray could not get there until the Friday evening but Vanessa had taken the day off in order that she and Gracia could set off early, arriving at midday. They spent the afternoon exploring the site and took a boat on the lake. Gracia had been a wonderful companion, according to Vanessa. But her mood had altered with the arrival of Gray. She became sullen and unresponsive, showing no inclination towards any of the activities they offered. On the Saturday night she had disappeared altogether after supper. Vanessa and Gray had searched for her and eventually Vanessa had found her lying near a pontoon fully clothed beneath a boy named Cory who was making a frightful hash of undoing her bra.

"Gracia!" Vanessa said gently. "You need to come back with me now." The pair disentangled.

"Is that your mum?" Cory asked.

"No way," Gracia replied and traipsed back to their chalet with Vanessa. "Do you have to tell Gray about Cory?" Gracia pleaded.

"No, I don't have to. But can you please make a bit more effort over this holiday, Gracia? It's not as if Gray and I would have come here anyway."

Gracia had undertaken to do so, but not kept her word.

"She was tired," said Gray after they had dropped her back at school. "Or she's hormonal, who knows?"

"No, Gray," Vanessa replied. "She's possessive. She can't help it. She's an only child after all. She and I, we get on OK. I think she quite likes me, actually. That's not the problem. She wants all of you. She doesn't want you to want anyone but her. When it's all three of us I force her to share your attention. She never had to share her parents, and you having a girlfriend is the last thing she wants. I'm a threat, Gray. Look, no-one could blame her for this. The poor girl, really. But as long as I'm around things are never going to get better. And to be honest, her possessiveness just stands totally in the way of us making a go of it, really, doesn't it? You don't have to make a choice between us. You have to put Gracia first, I have always understood that."

"But she'll learn to compromise," Gray had protested, "as she gets older. She's at a difficult age. And she's not here at all during term time?"

"Yes but when, Gray? It could be another ten years. I don't want to wait ten years before we make a real start of things. I don't think I can just be a term-time project for the foreseeable future." She put her hand on his arm then sighed. "Gray, I honestly don't think I'm being selfish, but you know, I'm thirty-seven. I can't wait forever."

"Vanessa and I have broken up," he said to Gracia during the next exeat.

She lolled sideways in his favourite chair with her legs hanging over one arm and glanced up.

"Oh. I wondered where she was. Why?"

"Irreconcilable differences is how you'd put it I suppose," he replied, sadly.

Gracia scowled. "Sounds very legal. What did you do wrong?"

Three years later Gray heard on the grapevine that Vanessa had married a doctor.

THE NEXT DAY – FRIDAY 5th APRIL 2019

ISLINGTON POLICE STATION

MORNING BRIEFING

"OK, listen up."

Detective Sergeant Ian Cartwright stood before the smart board at the top end of the briefing room and called his junior officers to attention. White painted walls around the room were plastered with mug shots of regular offenders and maps showing hot spots of local criminal activity. The volume of noise lowered as the shift turned its collective attention away from natter and gossip to the morning briefing. Some in the room swivelled on wheeled office chairs with an air of nonchalant confidence, others sat still and attentive, equally confident that, as members of the Metropolitan Police Service, they were up to whatever task lay ahead.

"Male body. Approximate age forty to forty-five found dead in Regent's Canal between Bridge Nos. 9 and 10 at approximately six am this morning by Amy Francis, a cyclist on her way to work. The search and recovery team are down there now. Initial signs are that the body had been in the water for less than twenty-four hours but pathology will confirm that. The body was clothed. Appearance: skin, facial hair, clothes and so on, suggest this was probably a tramp. Some personal effects, sleeping bag, rucksack etcetera have been recovered from beneath Bridge No. 9. Obviously at this stage we do not know if they belonged to the deceased. So ..."

Cartwright drew breath and wiped his brow. His morning routine had been interrupted by the early call to the Regent's Canal. He was keen to get tasks assigned then settle himself for the day with a cup of coffee. He continued.

"I've left uniform taking a statement from Ms Francis. Obviously, we now need to find out who the deceased was and how he died. Malek and Sanders, I want you two to go down there. There are no properties backing onto the canal in that area. It's Prince Albert Road on the north side and Regent's Park to the south so no scope for house to house enquiries. But there's plenty of pedestrian and cycle traffic along the canal path so I recommend you put up a witness appeal, see what comes in and take it from there. Meanwhile this end we need to set DNA matches in motion and sort out a media appeal. Detective Inspector Fraser is the senior investigating officer. As you know he is a man who does not like to waste time. Off you go Malek and Sanders. Play nicely."

ISLINGTON POLICE STATION TO PRIMROSE HILL

IMMEDIATELY AFTERWARDS

Jalal Malek watched his partner stride across the station car park and, without hesitation, approach the driver's door of their designated vehicle. She generally took the wheel when they travelled together and he preferred it that way. He had been taught to drive by his father, a cautious, double-checking kind of man and, whenever Jalal drove, Jayne criticised him for dithering. It was easier to give her control than to forbear her torrent of checks and commands from the passenger seat.

Jayne turned on the siren.

"What are you doing?" he asked.

"What does it look like?" she retorted.

"It's not an emergency. You can't put the siren on."

"Who says it isn't? There's a dead body, Jal. Could easily be an emergency."

She swung out to overtake a slow-moving line of traffic, heading directly towards a large lorry approaching from the other direction. The lorry glided into the side of the road in the nick of time as Jayne kept her foot firmly on the accelerator pedal and their vehicle continued to streak noisily ahead.

Heads turned. It was all Jalal could do not to cover his eyes.

At the T junction with York Way, Jayne was forced to draw to a halt. "What do you reckon? Left via Mornington Crescent or right and up round Camden?" she asked.

As Jalal deliberated, she turned right. To his relief she also turned off the siren. The traffic was heavy and their progress so far had been hazardous and stressful but no quicker than that of any other vehicle. He reckoned Jayne must have worked that out too, but he desisted from comment, hoping that the rest of the journey would be peaceful. Unfortunately, Jayne appeared motivated to explain herself. She went about it in a round about manner.

"We're different aren't we, you and I, Jal? I mean, no offence, but you're not really driven to win, are you? Whereas me, whenever I go anywhere, even if it's just a walk round to see my auntie with my sister, I want to get there first, know what I mean? Comes from all the athletics I did, I suppose. Did I tell you, I was under sixteens record holder for 10k when I was fourteen?"

"You did once, yes." Jalal replied. It was a triumph that Jayne had frequently mentioned.

"Sorry. But I'd have loved to have been a professional athlete," she mused. "No money in it though. What about you? This what you always wanted to do?"

Jalal could tell Jayne was only half listening as she negotiated her way towards their destination, but he told her anyway. Yes. He had formed the ambition to become a detective in his early teens as he sat alone watching TV police series night after night in his tiny bedroom in Sparkbrook, Birmingham. His parents, second generation immigrants from Kashmir, ran their own late night shop and were never in. Jalal was left in the charge of his elder sisters who practised make-up and beauty in their room next door.

"So how come you came to London?"

Jalal was surprised. Turned out Jayne was listening after all.

"My mom and dad thought they'd try and set up a balti house near Leyton, so we moved when I was sixteen." Although Jalal now spoke in mostly estuary tones, he'd never lost the bit of Brummie in him that insisted he refer to his mum as his mom.

And did they? Jayne was tapping an acrylic nail on the steering wheel. The car in front had stopped to let a woman with a pram and a toddler go over a zebra crossing. The toddler had dropped something en route, so everyone had to wait. Nevertheless, Jayne sounded sufficiently interested to allow Jalal to continue, even if only to pass the time.

"They tried but now they work in someone else's restaurant. It's easier really."

"What did they think when you said you wanted to join the police? Bet they were surprised."

Jalal considered this. "I suppose they were surprised. They were definitely proud. My mom worries though."

"Why?" A stretch of clear road appeared before them. Jayne moved from first to third gear and accelerated.

"Oh, you know." Jalal felt he had said enough. He could have told her that his mother worried about him getting into danger, about him being tired all the time, about the many and varied challenges which face officers in the modern police force, about him still being unmarried at the age of thirty-one. She worried that he came from a family whose genetic strengths were diligence and stoicism in the face of overt racism, rather than bravery or quick thinking and that he might one day buckle under the pressure of the job. He was her only son and the first member of the family to break the mould of doing menial work to scrape a living. So yes, his mom worried. But although he and Jayne had worked together on previous cases, they were not particularly close and to admit all of that might have made him seem somehow less of a man. He wished he hadn't mentioned his mother at all really. He changed the subject back to Jayne.

"What about you? Always lived round here?"

They were now on Prince Albert Road, just past Primrose Hill and Jayne was looking for a suitable side road in which to leave the car.

"Too right, I have. Born and bred, me. Here we are." She found a parking place and pulled in. "We can drop down onto the canal by the zoo I reckon. Can you get the witness appeal out of the back?"

And, without waiting for Jalal, Jayne set off purposefully towards the canal.

THE NEXT DAY – SATURDAY 6th APRIL 2019

MANCHESTER SQUARE, MARYLEBONE
10:30am

"It's nice to see you."

Gray greeted his niece. She had rung the previous evening to tell him that she was coming over. Standing inside his hall, she was petite, pretty, wearing no make-up. He wanted to hug her but didn't. She wasted no words on greeting and demanded:

"Have you heard from Patrick?"

He tried to sound as neutral as possible. "No, I haven't."

"There's no need to be judgmental."

"I wasn't, Gracia. I haven't heard from Patrick, no."

"Well, you don't have to worry. So, yes, we've been having an affair. Yes, we are both married. Yes, it was adultery. Yes, it was immoral. No, I don't regret it. Well not really. And yes, it is over, as you'd probably have told me it was always going to be. But nobody has got hurt. His wife didn't find out. Claudio didn't find out. No-one did. It's just, you know, over, okay?"

"I'm sorry."

"Don't lie."

"I'm sorry if you're hurt."

"I'm not hurt. Why do you think I'm the victim?"

"Do you want to talk about it?"

"No."

"Okay then. How about a cup of tea? Or coffee?" He assumed she'd refuse.

"Tea?"

They were still standing in the hall.

"Of course. Come with me while I make it."

She followed him into the kitchen and he set about attempting to assemble the wherewithal to make a pot of tea without testing her patience.

"Milk or sugar?"

"Just milk. Thanks."

"Come through."

They went into the snug. He sat down opposite her, sensing she had something to say.

"So?" he ventured.

She looked at him. He felt she was debating whether to raise the real issue or fob him off with something inconsequential.

"Something happened on Thursday night."

Gray put his teacup on the table beside him. "Go on."

She took a deep breath.

"Patrick and I were walking back to my flat along the canal. It was over. I'd finished it and it was over. Anyway, it doesn't matter. But we got into a bit of trouble. There was a sort of fight?"

"You had a fight?"

"No, not him and me. Him and someone else. A bloke. I don't know who he was. He looked like he was homeless or something. He kind of mugged us. Only he didn't 'cos he didn't seem to want anything. He just ran up and hit Patrick in the head and then his side and Patrick pushed him in the stomach and shoved him and the bloke fell down and then Patrick said we had to go and I didn't think we should just leave him because he was kind of just lying there. I mean he was conscious and everything, but you know. Anyway, I think Patrick thought he might attack us again or something so we ran away. But, look, I don't know if Patrick is going to go to the police or anything and I really don't want to talk to him. Or the bloke could say something, I mean I doubt he would but I don't know. But I can't be involved in this. I mean no way 'cos of publicity obviously. But, and I'm sure this won't happen, but if anyone asks, can you just say I was here all evening. Just in case. 'Cos, you know?"

She paused and drew breath. "Please?"

Gray put a finger to his temple, trying to absorb all this. She looked annoyed.

"Oh don't go all like that."

"Is Patrick hurt?"

Gracia shrugged.

"Not badly. Just bruises I think."

"What about the man?"

"A bit, I think. Patrick pushed him off and he fell over. He didn't get back up but he was definitely high."

It was all a bit much for Gray to absorb.

"Can you go through it again? A bit slower?"

She sighed and did so. When she'd finished he lifted his chin in thought and looked up.

"There wasn't anyone else around?"

"I don't think so."

"And the man didn't assault you in any way, just Patrick?"

"Yeah."

"Patrick pushed him off? He, the chap, fell over, and you both ran away?"

"Yes, pretty much. It was very quick. I don't know exactly. Do you have to ask so many questions?"

"I'm sorry, it's habit. I'm glad you got away before anything nastier happened. Look, I'm sorry if I'm being slow but why does it matter so much if you were there or not?"

"Because I was with Patrick, obviously."

Gray always forgot how careful she had to be about her public image. Her reaction rather begged the question why she'd taken the risk of having an affair in the first place. He decided to leave that aside.

"But no-one saw you, apart from the attacker?"

"Exactly. Just that. I wouldn't have bothered coming round but ... Look, actually this is fine. I'm just stressed. Don't worry about it. Sorry. Um." She edged forward in her chair.

Gray sensed her desire to leave and spoke kindly.

"Gracia, it's good of you to have told me about Patrick. I'm glad you're OK."

"Thanks."

Her look spoke gratitude. Love? He didn't kid himself. She walked towards the door.

"Thanks, Gray."

She hardly ever used his name.

THE NEXT DAY – SUNDAY 7th APRIL 2019

WEST HADDON, NORTHAMPTONSHIRE

10:30am

"See you later, darling. Enjoy your walk. I'll leave the gate open, shall I?" Jenny Kingdom shut the car door, pulled on her seat belt, engaged first gear and set off to church.

Patrick gathered leads, poo bags and dog treats from the utility room and called, "Billy! Bunter!"

A black and brindle tumble of stocky bull terrier/boxer cross breeds crashed downstairs and slid across the polished floor of the hall. "Mind Bunter's ear, you dimwits. Come on!"

The chestnut trees in the fields which lay on either side of the drive stood strong and ready for the blossom that would bounce on their branches in a month or so's time. Tiny spears of immature daffodils sprouted in the beds, pert and ready to flower, defiant in the face of frosts yet to come. The dogs ran ahead, shoulder-barging each other playfully. Usually Patrick loved to watch them but today a worry was nagging in his throat and spoiling the moment. He decided to get the phone call over with. At the end of the drive he shut the gate and rang Gray's number. Then he crossed the road to the footpath beyond. His walk across the fields to the next village and back would take about an hour and a half. He hoped the phone call would be shorter. After two rings, he heard Gray's voice.

"Patrick. Hello. I was hoping you would ring."

"Gray, I am deeply embarrassed. You know why, of course."

"Of course."

Gray's voice was reassuring. Patrick continued. "I owe you an explanation."

"No need, Patrick. Gracia came over yesterday."

"Did she?"

"She did. Patrick, please, we don't need to discuss this. There's no need. I imagine it was just a slip."

Patrick had expected stiff disapproval. The kindness in Gray's voice moved him to say more.

"Yes. Arguably the most stupid thing I've ever done in my life."

"We all make mistakes. I did too. I should not have forwarded the message to Gracia. I'm sorry."

Patrick stopped him.

"Please, Gray, there's no need for you to apologise. Did Gracia tell you that we have decided to go our separate ways?"

"She did, yes."

"I do want you to know this, Gray. It is important. Gracia was very dear to me. She still is. I don't think I ever hurt her. I do hope not."

"Thank you, Patrick. I am glad to hear that."

For the first time Patrick considered how Gray might be feeling.

"And, Gray, I hope you can understand why neither of us told you that we were, how can I put it, in a relationship. I think we both thought it would make things difficult for all of us."

There was a short silence. No one likes to be told they might make things difficult.

"Yes, Patrick I expect you're right. No, you are right. I do understand. I suppose I'm interested to know how long you've been – I mean when – I mean, I'm assuming my party?

Patrick owed him an explanation. "Yes." There was no need to elaborate.

"Does Jenny know?"

"No." Patrick was keen to move on. "Please accept my apology again though, Gray. It can't have been a welcome email."

"Oh, I don't know." A hint of humour. "It's not every day I'm told I'm being given a new nightie."

Patrick shuddered inwardly at the memory. He deserved it and didn't dare laugh.

Gray changed the subject slightly. "I gather you had a bit of trouble on the canal path? How are you?"

"She told you? Oh fine. Bit of a sore head, some bruises but nothing serious."

"Good. Yes, she did. Will you go to the police?"

"No. Not worth their time."

"Well that's probably best. Gracia was worried about it getting out. A news story like this would be very bad for her, she says. I don't think she need worry. I can't think that it will. This down and out, whoever he was, is hardly going to make a song and dance about it. What prompted it? Any idea?"

"None at all. Bugger just came at us from nowhere."

"On drugs?"

"Quite probably. With any luck he won't remember a thing."

"Well, there it is. So long as you are both all right. Nasty shock. But thank you for ringing, Patrick. I appreciate it."

"Good to talk, Gray. Be nice to have dinner, soon. I'll be in touch. Bye."

Patrick walked on. The dogs were sniffing around the base of a hedgerow. "Come on, you two." And he began to wonder what Jenny was going to cook for lunch.

THE NEXT DAY – MONDAY 8th APRIL

REGENT'S CANAL – BETWEEN BRIDGE NO. 9 AND PRIMROSE HILL BRIDGE

MORNING

Hip hop. The indomitable spirit and regular beat of the *Hamilton* soundtrack underscoring a good jog set James Mitchell up nicely for a day in court. His stride was well established and his breathing regular as he passed beneath the Blow-Up Bridge heading towards Regent's Park. A little further on, a short stretch of the path was cordoned off by police tape. They'd constructed a diversion onto the concrete upper path running parallel to the canal. Below the tape was a small metal A frame bearing a sign: Police. Witness Appeal. Did you see an accident here on ... *Thursday 4 April 2019 or Friday 5 April 2019 ...?* Please call 0207 111 1010.

On his way home, the same notice reminded him. He took a photo of it on his phone.

THE NEXT DAY – TUESDAY 9th APRIL

THE TEMPLE

9:00am

"Islington Police Station. Can I help you?"

James was at his desk in Chambers. "Is this the number I'm supposed to ring about an incident on Regent's Canal last Thursday?" he asked.

'Yes. Hold on a minute. I'll put you through."

He waited a few seconds then heard a male voice. "DC Malek. Can I help you?"

James rubbed his forefinger over his thumbnail, thinking carefully. "Um yes. I'm ringing in response to a notice I've seen on the path towards the west end of the Regent's Canal. I don't really have anything much to tell you and obviously I don't know what time the incident took place or anything, but I run along that stretch of canal most days. I saw the sign last night so I just thought I should ring and say that I was on the canal path last Thursday morning, and evening in fact. I was on my way to and from work."

He gave his name and contact details and explained that he worked in the Temple. Then he asked what had happened.

As he spoke, a clerk came into his room and stood just inside the door looking at James enquiringly. James pointed to the phone, held up five fingers to indicate how long he would be and the clerk went away.

Malek replied.

"Thank you, sir. We believe an incident took place some time between about two o'clock in the afternoon on Thursday 4th April and six o'clock the following morning. Unfortunately, the body of an adult male was found in the canal early on the Friday morning. Are you able to tell me approximately what time you were on the path in the evening, and where exactly?

James thought carefully.

"Thursday evening? I had a few things to do in Chambers after court so I must have left some time after six, then I got the tube to Baker Street. Obviously, it's not my nearest tube station but I quite often go home that way so I can run through Regent's Park and along the canal. So, I reckon I must have got onto the path by about quarter to seven, I'd say. There are two paths running parallel for a bit just after I get onto the canal at the zoo. You'll know that obviously. I took the lower path that runs alongside the water. I ran as far as Little Venice and then home. I saw nothing out of the ordinary at all. I hadn't been back there until yesterday when I saw your sign. So yes, on

Thursday evening roughly between say quarter to seven and half past, along the stretch of path between the zoo and Little Venice no, I saw nothing out of the ordinary. Did the man drown or what?"

Malek did not answer the question. His voice continued in a monotone.

"Did you see anyone on the canal path, sir?"

"Hardly anyone. I mean a few joggers, one or two people walking, that kind of thing."

"No one else?"

James suddenly remembered.

"Actually, yes. I did pass a colleague of mine. Patrick Kingdom. You might know him. He's a criminal silk. We said hello. Oh and he was with a woman. They were walking in the opposite direction to me, towards the zoo."

He was pressed for more detail about Patrick, which he gave. Then Malek asked him to describe the woman.

"I don't know, I didn't really take much notice. Small, dark, attractive. Mid 30s maybe. That's about it, really. She looked vaguely familiar, but I don't think she was anyone I know."

Malek thanked him for the information. James would have liked to have found out more but his clerk had appeared again, gesticulating almost incomprehensibly that before James left for court he was needed in the clerks' room. When he got there it turned out to be a matter that easily could have waited.

ISLINGTON POLICE STATION

11:00am

Detective Sergeant Ian Cartwright had been hoping to impress his DI with a rapid resolution of the case concerning the body found in the canal but everything seemed to be taking longer than necessary.

Cartwright was a heavy man who suffered from a combination of hypersalivation and large, fleshy lips which evidently lacked adequate sensation to alert him to the presence of crumbs and other debris which frequently adhered to them beneath mastic gobbets of spit. He had just enjoyed a sugar-coated almond croissant with his morning coffee.

A problem had arisen over the duty roster. He was a couple of detectives light. This did nothing to improve progress with the case nor his mood. His reassignment of duties had been interrupted by a request to see him from the two detective constables he had tasked to find out the circumstances surrounding the death of the man in the canal. They were standing before him now, hands behind their backs. Jalal Malek on the left. An experienced, reliable copper, solid. His partner, Jayne Sanders, interested Cartwright more. Attractive girl. Not even her uniform could disguise that. Tall, athletic, long dark hair pulled back into a tight bun. A bit headstrong but getting the hang of things. He had been pleased with the idea of putting them together. Malek the tortoise to Sanders's hare. It should be working well but they had yet to make much headway. Now what?

Ignorant of the fact that his mouth was flecked with icing sugar and one or two shards of nut, he listened with mounting irritation as Malek requested authority to interview a lawyer of some professional standing following a lead they had received from another lawyer, both apparently having been on the canal path during the evening before the body was found. Cartwright was not really attending to the detail. He wanted to get on with what he was doing. So, he sighed and with exaggerated patience he had said that yes, they had his authority to follow this and any other lead. Then he had begged their indulgence. Would they be kind enough not to ask him to hold their hand through every step of their investigation but perhaps draw on their own reserves of initiative and get on. And just in case he had not made himself clear he pointed out that he was in the job of policing not nannying. He dismissed them with an ultimatum that the case needed to be closed immediately after Easter. That gave them a fortnight.

As they departed, he licked his lips. To his greedy joy he discovered the pieces of slivered almond which he washed down with the dregs of his coffee and returned to his rosters. He was so focused on the excitement of his taste buds that he did not hear Sanders exclaim as the door to his office closed. "Great! Green light!"

TOP FLOOR FLAT, NORTH GATE MANSION BLOCK

EARLY EVENING

Patrick loathed the involuntary internal jolt that was invariably occasioned by the over-loud demand for attention of his front door buzzer. He lifted the receiver from the wall mount in the hall.

"Hello."

A male voice answered, "Is this Patrick Kingdom?" Unplaceable accent.

"Yes."

"We are Detective Constable Jalal Malek and Detective Constable Jayne Sanders of the Metropolitan Police."

Patrick was expecting them. "Hello. Come up."

He let them in. Their feet sounded heavy on the stairs. The male was tall and well built, thirtyish. His colleague was female, maybe a few years younger, dark haired, slimmer, attractive, expressionless. They showed their warrant cards.

"Come in." Patrick led them into the sitting room and indicated a sofa. The two officers perched. Their heavy, black clothing contrasted incongruously with Patrick's fine, light-coloured furnishings.

"Thank you for letting me know you were coming. How can I help?" Malek took the lead.

"As I explained when I rang earlier, sir, we are making enquiries in connection with an incident that might have occurred on or near the Regent's Canal last Thursday or Friday."

Patrick raised his eyebrows.

"Yes, you said. What's happened?"

Malek looked directly at him. The female did likewise.

"Unfortunately a body was found in the canal last Friday morning between Primrose Hill Bridge, that is the bridge just west of London Zoo, and the next bridge going further west, That's Bridge No. 9, Macclesfield Bridge, or the Blow-Up Bridge as it is sometimes called. Do you know where I mean?"

Thoughts crowded Patrick's mind. A body? What was this to do with him? Dead? Was this the man who had attacked him or was it someone else? His response was automatic.

"Er, yes I think so. Goodness! Do you know who it was?"

The female started to write notes in her pocket book. Malek's attentive look did not waver.

"Unfortunately not yet, sir. We are wondering if you can tell us if you were on the canal path at any time between Thursday afternoon and Friday morning?"

Patrick looked up to the ceiling, thinking.

"Um, let me think. Thursday. Yes, yes I was. I went for a walk up to the zoo that evening."

The female constable looked at him and resumed writing. Malek probed. "Why was that, sir?"

Keep Gracia out of this. Patrick told himself he had to do that. "I felt like a breath of fresh air, really I suppose. I'd been in court all day."

He hoped that 'in court' might alert them to his seniority in criminal matters and deter them from close questioning; that it might also distract them from the transparent untruth. Nothing about the cold, dull north London air of Thursday evening had invited a stroll up the canal.

Malek continued to press. "And what time was this, sir?"

The female constable started to scrape her biro up and down the page.

Patrick was grateful for the distraction.

"Has your pen run out? Hold on. I'll get you another."

He went into his study, glad of the breather. He returned with a new biro and handed it to her. She thanked him.

Malek continued.

"You were saying you went for a walk on Thursday evening. At what time was that, sir?"

"Around half six, quarter to seven. Maybe a bit later."

"Is that the time you left here?"

"Um yes, I left here at, well I don't know really, say around a quarter to seven and got back at maybe half seven."

"And you didn't see anything unusual?"

Should he tell them about the attack? Someone had apparently died but that was nothing to do with him, surely. Keep it simple.

"No. I saw nothing unusual."

The female DC wrote.

Malek continued.

"Were you on your own, sir?"

Keep Gracia out of it. Imperative. "Yes."

"Were there many people on the path at that time?"

"One or two. A few. Not many. A lot of people walk that way after work. There are usually some joggers. It rather depends on the weather."

"But on Thursday evening it was rather cold?"

"Yes, as I discovered. I should have taken a warmer coat. I remember thinking that."

Patrick was beginning to relax as he found the story easier to tell. Malek had another question.

Did you see anyone you knew?

Both officers looked at him.

"No, I don't think so. Oh no, wait, yes I did. James Mitchell. He is a barrister. We are in the same Chambers. He was coming the other way."

"Yes sir. Actually we have spoken to Mr Mitchell. He was under the impression that you were walking with another person."

Shit.

"Really?"

"Yes sir."

"No. I think he's got that wrong. I was on my own."

But he had no choice but to account for Gracia. Damn James Mitchell.

"Oh no, actually there was someone else."

The female constable stopped writing, looked up at him expectantly, then down again, pen poised. Patrick thought fast.

"A woman. She stopped me to ask the best place to leave the canal to get to Chalk Farm tube station. I was going that way so we walked together to Primrose Hill Bridge. That was her quickest route."

Malek took a deep breath then exhaled.

"I see. Thank you. So, to summarise – you left here at about six forty-five?"

"Well around then. I'm not sure exactly what time it was."

Malek looked to his colleague. "Let's say approximately."

"Yes."

"And walked along the canal path as far as the zoo and then came back here. You didn't see anyone you knew apart from Mr Mitchell and you were accompanied by an unknown woman for a short distance. Apart from that nothing out of the ordinary occurred. You got home at approximately seven-thirty pm. Is that it?"

"Yes."

Surely that would be all. It was not. Malek had more.

"Can you describe the woman?"

"Shortish, slim, dark hair, late twenties."

"Can you remember what she was wearing?"

He shook his head. "No I'm sorry, I really can't." He looked at the female DC. Her eyebrows raised a fraction as she continued to write.

"Thank you sir. Well, I think that's all."

The constables looked at each other in agreement. But Patrick could not let them just leave. He had to know.

"May I ask something?"

"Yes sir."

"Was it male or female, the body?"

"Male, sir."

"Do you know who it was?"

"Not as yet sir, no. We are still making enquiries."

"Young? Old?"

"We don't have all the details, sir."

Patrick continued to talk. Now the tricky bit seemed to be over, he wanted to sound helpful.

"Well, I hope you find out who he is soon. There may be a very worried family somewhere."

"Indeed sir. Thank you for seeing us."

The officers looked at each other and rose to their feet.

"Please keep me informed. I'd like to know if you find out who he was?"

Malek looked curious.

"Really, sir? Why is that?"

Patrick couldn't think of a single valid reason, but had to say something, for God's sake.

"Well I suppose there's a chance he might be local. A lot of my neighbours take that walk. I wouldn't want to say the wrong thing to anyone."

He tried not to blink as he looked from one to the other and asked himself how he could have said something so fatuously stupid.

Malek resumed, "I don't think you will need to worry about that, sir. We'll leave you to the rest of your evening now. Thank you for your time."

They left. Patrick opened the fridge and reached for the gin. "Bloody hell," he muttered. After all, he was the one who was supposed to be good at cross examination. That DC was good. Fuck. He should have just told the truth. Should he ring Gracia? No, he hadn't mentioned her name, maybe that was for the best, no need. What about Gray? No. James Mitchell? Yes. See what he had to say.

OUTSIDE NORTH GATE MANSION BLOCK, ST JOHN'S WOOD

A MOMENT OR TWO LATER

Malek stretched his seat belt around him and clicked it in. "What did you reckon?"

"Classic!" Jayne Sanders laughed. It was not the reaction Malek was expecting.

"Go on."

"Very smooth. Very cool. But he was sweating man. See his armpits? Gross. I dunno, Jal. Hasn't taken things much further though, has it? Has there been any more response to the witness appeal?"

Jalal shook his head. "Nothing. I just thought it was odd that he was so interested in who the deceased was." It was his turn to mimic. *I just wouldn't want to say the wrong thing.* I mean, come on."

Jayne laughed. Jalal's attempt to imitate Kingdom had landed somewhere in a posh part of the West Midlands. "Any progress on ID yet?"

"No. Shouldn't be long. I'll chase them up. Know what, I'm starving."

He opened the glove compartment, revealing an ancient roll of extra strong mints which he picked up and examined suspiciously.

Jayne laughed. "Enjoy!"

LITTLE VENICE

THE SAME TIME

It's been there ages. It's not like I've drunk all that today. Sake!"

Jake Mitchell, fourteen years old, six-foot, face bright red through a combination of anger and excessive use of acne astringent, stood one side of the kitchen table and railed at his father who stood opposite him in suit and silk tie, brandishing a half-full bottle of vodka. Behind the boy, French windows gave onto a mock Italian garden: gravel, miniature box hedges, a little fountain and a pair of imitation renaissance lover statues found in a side street shop in Pisa. Subtle ground-level lights gave an effect of calm and beauty which was totally at odds with the scene playing out in the kitchen. Carrie Mitchell, Jake's mother, a relationship counsellor with a peaceful temperament and the perfect skill set required for calming family conflict silently chopped onions and peppers beside the cooker.

Jake's father, James, wished she had handled the situation herself and not involved him.

The boy hurled another verbal grenade.

"And what are you doing searching around my room anyway? Don't you have anything better to do? You are such a loser."

"Such" was delivered two octaves above the rest of the sentence, Jake's voice being unreliable. The effect was often hilarious. On this occasion James, incensed by his son's rudeness, was in no mood to laugh.

"I have plenty better to do, Jake. Jelena found it under your bed. I'll spare you the embarrassment of hearing what else she found. How long has it been there?"

"I don't know. A month? What's Jelena doing messing around in my room anyway?"

"What do you think? What we pay her for: cleaning. For God's sake, Jake. Vodka? You're fourteen years old. Where did it come from?"

"I don't know."

Basso profondo. James sang in a local amateur choir and not for the first time fleetingly thought Jake might have a good singing voice if he would only get off his arse and give it a go. He returned to combat.

"Don't lie to me. You're in enough trouble."

"I'm not lying, I don't know. I can't remember."

"Oh, so buying bottles of vodka has become such a routine thing you don't remember where you got it?"

"I didn't buy it."

"Who did then?"

"I can't remember. I. Just. Told. You."

A blind alley. Unfazed, James deployed the advocate's strategy of changing tack without loss of momentum.

"Are there any more? If we go through your room will we find more bottles hidden about, or is this the only one? I don't believe this, Jake. What do you do, have a slug before you go to sleep?"

"You are so hypocritical."

"So" hit another stratospheric note. But Jake had scored a hit and now James was losing it.

"What?!"

"You drink way too much. You're always saying you do. And you're the one in the christening photo pouring champagne into my baby bottle. So whose fault is it that I drink now? Have you thought about that?"

James left the kitchen. The urge to punch his towering child was becoming irresistible. Jake's voice followed him.

"See! You've got no answer, have you?"

Carrie came out to him in the hall.

"James, calm down. There's no point getting so angry. We need a bit of perspective on this."

"You talk to him then."

His phone vibrated in his back pocket. "Bloody hell."

Carrie returned to the kitchen and James shut the door to mute her attempts to pacify their indignant son who was moving on to accusations of invasion of privacy and breach of human rights.

James looked at his phone to see who was calling. Patrick Kingdom. He'd have to take it.

"Patrick. How are you?"

"Good, good. Yes, good. Have I rung at a bad time? You sound out of breath."

James leaned his back against the wall separating the kitchen from the hall and looked upwards. A large cobweb spanned a corner of the ceiling. He must remember to tell Carrie to instruct Jelena to get rid of it. It did not occur to him to do it himself.

"No, it's fine. How can I help?"

"Well, I've just had the police round about this body they found in the canal the other day. Following up on your information. Good man, by the way. The two who came to see me didn't have any details of who it was or anything, apart from that it was male. I was just wondering if you know any more?"

James could hear Carrie's gentle voice from the kitchen trying to reason with the erratic cadences of their son's objections. He spoke as he walked down the hall toward to the sitting room. The door was slightly ajar.

"No, I don't really. I don't get the impression the police do either."

Table lamps lit a comfortably furnished room. A documentary about Hasidic Jews was on the TV. Sixteen-year-old Eve, lying full length on a sofa in her school uniform, looked at him in annoyance and held her forefinger to her lips. "Shh. I'm watching this," then with emphasis, "For. School."

James left the room closing the door behind him and returned to the hall to sit on the stairs.

"I hope this hasn't put you out, Patrick. I'm rather surprised they followed it up, actually. I should think they're finding tramps in the canal all the time. I hope they didn't come at a bad time."

Patrick sounded surprised.

"A tramp? Really? Did they say that?"

James felt a sharp blow to the side of his head. His elder daughter, Emily, had knocked it with her knee as she endeavoured to climb past him to get down the stairs into the hall. She opened the sitting room door and walked in, then yelled to her sister, "Get off!! That's where I sit."

James rubbed his head as he got up to shut the door and close off the sound of the scuffle that had broken out.

"Sorry. A tramp? Oh, I don't know. Maybe I just assumed. I might have got that wrong. There was a cellophane wrap of flowers by the police witness appeal when I went by there this morning. It looked rather pathetic. Maybe that's why. Anyway, all I could tell them was what time I was there and that I'd seen you. I'm afraid I didn't know the name of the person you were with?"

James fell silent, hoping to be told. He enjoyed his reputation for being the first to know good gossip. This could be promising. Patrick's explanation, "Oh no, nor did I. She wanted to know the way to Chalk Farm tube so she walked along with me for a while," struck him as possibly a little thin but nothing to get his teeth into.

A crescendo from the kitchen indicated that his wife's attempts to reason with their son were failing while noises from the sitting room indicated that his daughters had reached no agreement over who could sit where or what to watch on the TV.

"Listen I'd better go, Patrick. We've got World War Three going on here at the moment. Teenagers. Remember?"

"Of course. I'll let you go. Bye."

He walked into the kitchen, ignored Jake and Carrie, opened the French windows and stepped out into the garden. Water caught the light as it ran in a soft stream from the fountain. If only he had a drink.

EIGHT DAYS LATER – MAUNDY THURSDAY 18th APRIL

THE ROYAL COURTS OF JUSTICE

8:45am

"Good Morning."

Gray showed his card to the security guards in the booth. They opened the automatic door and he stepped into the cold austerity of the side entrance to the Royal Courts of Justice. The only decoration in the stone stairwell leading to the judges' corridors was a series of heavy, ancient portraits of their robed forebears. Gray's room was on the second floor. A wooden, glass-windowed door swung into it. Beyond lay deep-red carpet and a degree of warmth. A large, hand-painted name plate set within a wooden frame designated Gray's room. 'Mr Justice Andrew'. Gracia had come here once. She'd told him that it looked as if all the judges had been given the same Christian name.

"Very funny. It's the job title."

"I knew that."

Today Neil was already in the room. He had been Gray's clerk and constant work companion for the two years since Gray's appointment to the High Court Bench. Neil's job was that of glorified PA. It included liaison with the various courts in which Gray sat, as well as responsibility for all professional and social engagements that Gray was expected to fulfil.

The work alternated in six weekly cycles. Civil work in London during which they worked at the Royal Courts of Justice then a stint on circuit during which Gray presided over serious criminal trials at a Crown Court somewhere in the provinces. During the London-based periods Neil lived with his family in Kew. On circuit, he would travel with Gray and they would both be accommodated in judges' lodgings. These were large, private, staffed houses owned and maintained by the Ministry of Justice which afforded security and a stress-free environment to which High Court judges were able to retire after a day's sitting.

When other judges and their clerks were in residence, Gray and Neil spent barely any time together after the close of the court day. Clerks ate and relaxed in separate rooms which were not as formal as those used by the judges. But when Gray was the only judge in lodgings he preferred to socialise with Neil rather than enjoy splendid isolation. They would eat together and sometimes they would go to the pub or a football match. There had been one unforgettably thrilling game when Preston North End (Neil's team) had beaten Brighton (Gray's) in a cup tie. The two men were comfortable together and acquainted with the complications of each other's personal lives. Both were polite, reliable, discreet, correct.

"Good morning, sir. Coffee?"

"Thank you, Neil."

Neil went next door to his own room, marked 'Clerk to Mr Justice Andrew'.

Gray sat at his desk and logged onto his computer. His plan for the day was to finish writing a judgment. It would be good to get it done before Easter. As he read through the paragraphs he had written so far, Neil brought in a cup of coffee and placed it carefully on Gray's desk. Then, uncharacteristically, Neil hovered.

"I'm sorry, sir. There's something I think you should see."

He took his mobile phone from his pocket, and showed Gray the screen. It displayed an image of two bare-fleshed and wide-mouthed women sitting in a taxi on either side of a handsome, dark, curly-haired man, unmistakably Claudio. He was also smiling. One woman's arm lay along the back seat, her hand on his neck, fingers evidently entwined in his curls. The other woman's hand was on his thigh. The headline read:

'Gracia Peel Husband Caught In Rome Sex Romp'.

GLOUCESTER AVENUE, PRIMROSE HILL

MID MORNING

Gracia leant out of bed to check the time. She flopped her hand onto her phone which lay on the floor. She thanked God it was morning and that she had been spared the middle of the night hours of wakefulness that periodically tormented her. Before opening her eyes she had been thinking about how she might spend the day ahead. It had been an unrewarding exercise.

Looking forward to seeing Patrick had become an enjoyable guilty pleasure. She was discovering that adjustment to the loss of anticipation was a slow process. Devising distractions was exhausting.

Why had she admitted Patrick into her life, she asked herself. She had a younger, attractive husband, after all. Claudio was a man who, when he looked at her, made her feel that she was the most beautiful, fascinating woman in the world. Foolishly, when they had first met she had believed that look. Every predictable truism described their courtship, or whirlwind romance as she bitterly reviewed it. She had been intoxicated with the lifestyle that an Italian lakeside summer suggested might last forever, culminating in a fairy tale wedding surrounded by his adoring family who cooed and clucked around her in a language she did not understand.

It was only after they were married that she realised that that was the look he bestowed on all attractive women. More significantly, that it was calculated to make every female object of his attention feel unique. Was Claudio faithful to her? She had to assume not, but had never had proof.

So, the question was not so much why Patrick, as why Claudio? The one thing that Claudio did exceptionally well was complement her image. They looked good together. And since he did, at least, allow her to believe in the possibility of love by affording her the courtesy of lingering looks and attention when he was present, there was no need to muddy her life or image with divorce.

Why Patrick then? Sometimes she really thought he loved her too. Good enough reason. His way with her was more paternal. He allowed her to be a child, merely raising an eyebrow when even she knew she was being impossible. And the fact that he had his own wife and family gave them both protection against making bigger, life-changing decisions regarding their future. They could live in the moment. Patrick was handsome, they had fun, he made her feel good about herself and hey, what was not to like about forbidden fruit? Fine, he may not have been a long-term prospect, but she had learned long ago that long-term prospects weren't all they were cracked up to be.

Six months into their relationship she had asked if she could watch him in court. His reply had been nonchalant. "If you want to. It's a public arena. Anyone can go." So she had sat for an afternoon listening to him debate a matter of law with his opposite number and the judge. It was an obscure but apparently pivotal point that Gracia could not follow. But, visually, Patrick was a delight. He stood over six feet two inches tall. His robes hung from his shoulders adding elegance to his bearing. The curls of his greying hair around the edges of his wig lent an attractive aspect to his overall appearance which was authoritative. Gracia found the net effect enjoyably arousing. Regular recall of it was a habit she needed to kick. She was doing her best.

At the start of the week her agent had told her that filming of the new series of *Initiate* had to be delayed by a month because the director had fallen ill. Accordingly, Gracia now had a vista of unwanted free time. She picked up her phone. After a quick check on personal messages which conveyed nothing of particular interest, she gave in to another guilty pleasure and opened the Daily Mail online app and clicked on to UK Showbiz for celebrity gossip. Who'd done what of interest in the last twenty fours? '**Gracia Peel Husband Caught In Rome Sex Romp**' was the headline story.

"Are you kidding me?"

She fell back onto her pillow in impotent frustration, raised her phone again and scrolled for Claudio's number but then did not call it. What was the point? The damage was done now. She had no time for grovelling half-truths from him. The phone display lit up as she held it. Gray. The last person she felt like talking to. OK not the last. Claudio was the last. Gray wouldn't know about Claudio though. He only read The Times, didn't he? She'd keep it as brief as possible.

"Hello, Gray."

"Gracia, I'm sorry to be the bearer of bad news but I've seen something unfortunate in the press. I thought you should know about it."

Pause. Sigh. "I already do."

"Oh. Have you spoken to Claudio?"

"Not yet."

"Oh. Well I'm sure there won't be any truth in it."

"Are you? I'm not."

"My dear. This must be upsetting."

"Bloody embarrassing, more like." She felt her throat constrict. "It's just so ... oh, I don't know." Tears ran down her cheek. She sniffed and tried to regain composure. "Sorry. I'm fine."

"Would you like to come over tonight?"

She began the routine excuse. "No it's okay. I've got to work on the new ..." But then she paused to consider the prospect of spending the evening with Gray. The scenario appeared warm and comforting. She wouldn't have to explain anything and he had already shown that he could be surprisingly unjudgmental, for a judge. "Although actually, no, I suppose I could really. What time?"

"Whenever you like. I'll cook something. What do you eat nowadays: Vegetarian? Vegan? Meat? Fish?

"Anything."

"Righto. See you later."

Gracia put the phone back down on the floor and curled into a ball beneath her duvet. Two hours later she looked at her phone again. Four missed calls from Claudio. One from Patrick.

She got up, showered, dressed, drank a strong black coffee and took another look at her phone. She could happily ignore Claudio but the missed call from Patrick beckoned. She couldn't help herself. She returned the call.

THE TEMPLE

LUNCHTIME

Chicken, avocado and basil. Patrick was alone in his room in Chambers. A large window looked out onto the pavement outside. The room was cleanly decorated in pale colours, the walls lined with shelves bearing uniformly bound volumes of Law Reports. He had unpackaged his sandwich and just taken the first large bite when the phone rang.

"Gracia. How are you?"

"Are you eating?" Her tone was aggressive, accusatory.

He chewed and tried to swallow quickly but he couldn't make the bread go down and his "Sorry, just a second." came out as an inarticulate gargle.

"Why did you ring me?" she demanded.

Typical of her to be so abrupt. He had hoped to introduce the reason for ringing more gently. Finally, he swallowed.

"I've had the police round."

He pushed the rest of his sandwich aside and nervously began to fiddle with a heap of paper clips that lay on his desk, placing them carefully one on top of another.

"Why?"

Two paper clips became inseparably linked. He tried to disentangle them, failed, then ceased fidgeting, closed his eyes and leant forward on his desk to focus carefully on how to choose his words.

"I don't know if you know this already but a man's body was pulled out of the Regent's Canal a couple of weeks ago. It was the morning after you and I, well you know. The police came to see me a couple of days later because that chap James who we bumped into, I don't know if you remember, saw a police witness appeal on the canal path. He is a decent sort of chap so he rang and told them he'd passed by. He didn't see anything but he mentioned he'd seen me there too so they wanted to know if I could help in any way."

He leaned back in his chair and closed his eyes as he waited for her reaction. Her voice remained unnervingly level.

"What kind of body?"

"A man. That's all I knew at first. But they came back to see me again yesterday evening with some more information."

"They've been to see you twice?"

"Yes. Like I say, last week and then again yesterday evening."

Gracia's voice was cold in response.

"How come?"

"Well, partly to tell me who he was. I had asked them to keep me informed.

His name was David McBrain. Forty-three. No-one has come forward to identify him but they've been able to find out who he was from his DNA because he had a criminal record. Bit of an odd one, nothing till he was in his mid-thirties then a GBH. Must have been a nasty one. He got eight years."

Gracia made the obvious connection. Her voice remained flat. "Is it the man who attacked us?"

"I am afraid so. They showed me a photograph. It was one from their records, but it's him, yes."

"But he can't have died. How come? He was fine when we left him, just a bit hurt, not dying for God's sake. We'd have known."

Common ground. Thank God. He crossed the room to sit on the cast iron radiator beneath the window.

"Quite. I just took the wind out of his sails, I'm sure of it. Apparently, the pathology shows a couple of bruises, cuts on the front and back of his head, he'd broken his wrist, various other minor cuts. His lungs were full of water. They believe he drowned."

"Did this James person, whoever he was, say that I was with you?" The question he was dreading.

"Gracia, he did, I'm afraid."

He hurried to continue before she interrupted.

"But, don't worry, he did not know who you were and I told them you were just a passer-by asking for directions."

"What did you actually say?"

"Simply that. I said that I was walking beside the canal and that a woman stopped me and asked for directions to Chalk Farm tube station so I walked with you, or her as I put it, for a bit as I was going that way too."

"Why didn't you tell them about the bloke who hit you?"

"Because there's every chance that had nothing to do with this."

Gracia fell silent. He continued.

"And it was the easiest way of keeping you out of it, Gracia."

"I don't see why, but carry on."

Patrick couldn't withhold any longer the remainder of what Malek and Sanders had told him the previous evening. He returned to his chair and sat forward once more, his elbows on his desk, pushing the paper clips further out of his sight as he concentrated.

"It's just got a bit more complicated. They told me last night they've got CCTV of us near the crossing on Prince Albert Road between the zoo and Primrose Hill. Apparently, I rub my side or something and it looks like we're talking. You go off across Primrose Hill and then I walk back along the road.

"What's wrong with that?"

"Why wouldn't I walk back along the path?"

"Cos you don't want to bump into the psycho who's just attacked you?"

"But they don't know about that."

"Then tell them."

"But that could, well, complicate things, and bring you into it."

"Why? You said you were with a passer-by. They don't need to know it was me."

He could tell she wasn't in the mood for collaboration. He needed to think. Maybe she was right and he should tell the police about the attack. But what reason could he give for not having mentioned it before? And now the bloke who attacked them has been found dead. An enquiry into a suspicious death is only a step away from a murder enquiry once it is discovered that the victim has been in a fight. He spoke carefully.

"Well, that is something I am going to have to think about. I have told them I need to see the CCTV footage. I'm going to Islington Police Station tomorrow. It may not be us at all. But if it is, Gracia, listen I don't want to find myself suspected of this chap's murder. If I'm going to tell them about the attack I need you to say you were with me, so you can tell them what happened?"

She did not hesitate.

"One hundred per cent not, Patrick. I'm not going to risk everything to get you out of this mess you've created. If you say I was there, it's not going to help you, it'll just land me in trouble as well. I'm a suspect then too, aren't I? If you say it was me I'll deny it. Absolutely no fucking way."

She hung up. Patrick checked the time. "Shit."

He had fifteen minutes to get back to the Old Bailey. It usually took twenty. He hurried from his room, leaving his sandwich dying on his desk.

MANCHESTER SQUARE, MARYLEBONE

7:30pm

Gray sprinkled parmesan cheese over the top of the lasagne and covered it with a tea towel so that when Gracia arrived he could put it in the oven and focus on her. He looked at the sink. He had used almost every pot, frying pan and dish that he owned and they lay in the plastic washing up bowl alongside tiny floating squares of onion and strands of béchamel sauce. The quantity of pots required was a factor he always forgot when he decided to make lasagne. He rolled up his sleeves to begin to arrange them. The doorbell rang three times, urgently.

Gracia. Crying. Swearing. She pushed past him, wrenching a short black wig from her head and sunglasses from her face. He followed.

"Whatever's happened?"

She stood at the kitchen sink, gripping the edge with both hands, breathing heavily, then turned on the tap and poured a glass of water.

"Fucking paps. Why can't they fucking leave people alone?"

Gray was astounded. He had never known a photographer set foot near his house.

"Here?"

She turned to face him.

"No. Outside the Chiltern fucking Firehouse. I don't even think it was me they were after. I was just walking past. God, I'm so stupid! Why didn't I think?"

"Did they speak to you?"

"No they never do. They just get a burst of pictures and fuck off. They'll sell it easily. That's all the tabloids want. So now instead of this fucking Claudio story just going away it'll carry on tomorrow too and the producers are just going to love me for that. I might as well withdraw from this series now." She took a large mouthful of water and turned to refill her glass. "Your sink is disgusting, by the way."

Gray had not the faintest idea what to say to make this situation appear better than Gracia feared. He knew nothing about how film producers or the paparazzi operated. He stood silently for a moment then lifted the bottle he had opened earlier.

"Let's sit down and talk it through with this."

Gracia looked grateful. She took off her boots and followed him through to the snug.

Gray had a thought.

"I suppose one way of looking at this is that it is positive attention as far as you are concerned. If Claudio has misbehaved, it doesn't reflect badly on you. If anything, your fans will love you all the more, Gracia. You haven't done anything wrong."

Gracia pondered. "Suppose not."

Gray filled her glass then turned to walk to his own chair. "Have you spoken to him?"

She looked sullen. "No. He's tried to ring but what's the point? He'll deny it. He may be lying, he may not. It doesn't matter. I'm not likely to find out the truth by talking to him, am I?"

Gray decided it was best to let her leave it at that.

Gracia had tucked her feet beneath her on the ample, plump-cushioned armchair. Her left elbow was leaning on the arm, her hand behind her head, fingers twiddling long strands of creamy blonde hair. She drank then gently tipped the glass to watch the surface tilt from side to side as she spoke.

"My agent agreed with the producers that the best thing was to put out a statement saying I have no comment."

Gray sensed she knew that from a professional viewpoint her situation was not as damaging as she had first feared.

She drained her glass and held it out to him. "It's all a bit shit really, isn't it? Is there any more?"

As he went into the kitchen, Gray wondered whether to tell her that Patrick had rung. He returned with the bottle and the conclusion that it was too soon. Their conversation turned to the delay in filming and how she might spend her time.

After a while they ate. The lasagne turned out well and Gracia's mood appeared to brighten. Only periodically would her brow crease for some moments as she appeared to lapse into a moment of anxiety. As time passed, Gray sensed her relax and felt that this was the best moment to introduce his subject. He spoke casually.

"Patrick rang me after you came round last week." She sat up, instantly alert.

Too soon.

"When?"

"The next day."

"What did he say? You could have told me."

Back foot.

"He just wanted to apologise for the email. Really that was fine. It was a mistake and none of my business. I should have ignored it. I am sorry. But I thought you'd want to know. I wasn't sure when it would be best to tell you."

To his surprise she began to weep. He had never known how to react when this happened.

"Oh dear, what is it?" She struggled to speak.

"He is such a prick. Why do all the men in my life behave like fucking dicks?"

All the men? Let it go. He tried to reassure her.

"I barely looked at the email. I wouldn't even know what it said now. You needn't worry about it."

She interrupted. Anger defeated self-pity.

"I don't mean that. I mean, yes, that was him being a dick too. It's the fact he was so fucking careless. You could have been anyone. I do NOT need some wanker around me messing my life up by twatting off tacky emails to all and sundry."

All and sundry? Let it go.

"So I finished it. He didn't even seem to mind that much so thank God I did, actually because playing back-up to the wife in a big house in the country isn't that much fun and that was never going to change. Do you know what? We NEVER ate out. OK perhaps that was partly my choice too, but Deliveroo and a shag is not quite the heady mix I've been waiting for all my life."

He hoped she would not descend to further detail.

She continued. "So, fuck it, done, over. Get on with my life. Then the fucking director of *Initiate* gets mumps or some stupid thing, and NOW, it turn out that fucking PATRICK has told a whole lot of lies to the police about the thing that happened on the canal path because the bloke who attacked us somehow ended up in the bloody canal and his body was pulled out the next day, NOT that that was anything do with us, OBVIOUSLY, but NOW, JUST in case he's charged with murder or some crap, Patrick wants me to throw myself under the bus with him and say I was there! No fucking way. He probably wants me to say that we'd been having an affair too, just in case me being involved in a murder isn't quite enough to interest the press. Honestly Gray, what's WRONG with everyone?"

Gray shook his head in disbelief. "What? Who has died? Patrick's done what?"

Gracia's shoulders sank. She sighed exasperatedly and stood up. "Oh, you talk to him."

She walked to the door. "I'm going to bed."

She hadn't asked if her old room still had a bed in it. She hadn't asked if she could stay. As she left the room she turned.

"Is there a towel?"

Gray spoke kindly. "On the bed." It was too late to ring Patrick.

GOOD FRIDAY 19th APRIL

PLAISTOW, EAST LONDON

2:00am

"Who are ya! Who are ya!" Charlie Kingdom chanted mockingly, as his elder brother's goalkeeper threw himself the wrong way and watched helplessly as the ball crashed into the back of the net. His teammates returned robotically to the centre circle while Charlie's crowded around each other in virtual celebration.

Rob Kingdom threw his controller to Charlie's bedroom floor and pointed accusingly at the TV screen in front of them protesting "What did he do that for? Moron!"

"Three nil!" Charlie's jubilant mocking was relentless.

The game resumed. Rob's midfielders kept the ball efficiently to themselves but their comeback was confounded by the final whistle. He pushed his chair back from the desk in his room, put his hand behind his brother's head and roughed his hair.

"Fine, you win." Then he yawned and checked his phone. "Man! Seen what the time is?"

Charlie checked his own phone and snorted in amusement. They had been playing Fifa for three solid hours. The plan had been to have one quick game before bed then get up in the morning to drive home to Northamptonshire for Easter.

Rob stood up, yawned and stretched, then hooked his finger through the handles of the two coffee mugs.

"I'll put the dishwasher on. What time shall we leave in the morning? Doesn't have to be early, does it?"

Charlie had kept himself on high alert in his effort to beat his brother and was not remotely tired.

"Why don't we go now?"

"Fuck off."

"No, think about it. There'll be no traffic now. The motorways will be rammed tomorrow. We could do it in a couple of hours, easy."

"But I'm knackered, aren't you?"

"Weirdly, no, I'm fine actually. Mum will think it's great. She'll get up thinking we're not coming till the evening and we'll be there already. I've got a key so we don't have to wake her up. Come on. It'll be fun. We can pick up some energy drinks for the journey. Easy drive and then we can sleep all day at home if we want to."

"So, we don't tell Mum we're coming?"

"No, we'll just be there when she gets up. She'll think it's great. She gets another whole day of us."

"What about Dad?"

"He's probably not getting home till the evening."

"But I haven't packed." Rob. Ever practical.

"Nor me. Won't take long though. How about we leave in half an hour, forty-five minutes?"

"OK then. I'm pretty tired bro. I mean I can drive for a bit, I suppose." Rob sounded doubtful, but willing.

"Great." Charlie was pumped and ready for this latest brotherly escapade. "See you by the car in thirty, OK?"

ISLINGTON POLICE STATION

9:00am

It had been a while since Patrick had smelt the clinical odour of cheap disinfectant solution that lingers around many police stations. It had reminded him of the early years when, as a junior barrister, he had had to make early morning visits to police cells to take instructions from prisoners arrested overnight in order to make bail applications when they went up before the magistrates.

Stepping outside, he took a gulp of air then emptied his lungs.

DC Sanders had met him at the front desk and greeted him formally. Patrick had responded in kind and was led to a plain, sparsely furnished interview room where DC Malek sat behind a table on which sat a TV monitor. Sanders offered tea. Patrick refused and watched Malek set up the equipment to play the CCTV recording as Sanders sat down next to her partner, pulled a notebook towards her and took out her pen.

"All right for ink?" Patrick attempted to be jovial. She acknowledged the joke with a tepid smile and sat back as Malek explained that the recording camera was fixed to a lamp post on Prince Albert Road at the top of a slope which led up from the canal. The camera was focused on the pedestrian crossing to Primrose Hill.

Patrick had viewed many CCTV recordings and was well-accustomed to their appearance. Still, black and white images jumped from frame to frame creating the impression of an early silent film. Technology had come this far! Two people walked into shot from the direction of bottom left then stopped and stood on the pavement close to the crossing. Patrick immediately recognised himself and Gracia. His face was towards the camera. She stood opposite him with her back to it, facing Primrose Hill.

The images showed Patrick rub his side and touch his head. After thirty seconds, Gracia took the crossing over the road to Primrose Hill. She did not look back. Patrick turned to his left and walked out of shot, apparently along Prince Albert Road towards St John's Wood. The time on the recording was 19:20.

Patrick confirmed that the man was himself and that the woman was the one he had met on the towpath. He said that he had no recollection of why he had touched his side or head.

Malek went back to the start.

"You took the lower path alongside the canal from Bridge No. 8 to Primrose Hill Bridge, that is Bridge No. 10 which links Primrose Hill to Regent's Park at the zoo, is that right?"

"Correct."

"And how long would that walk normally take you, do you think?"

Such a simple question. How long had it taken? Patrick flanneled. "I don't know. I have never timed it."

"And the woman? Which direction was she walking in?"

"When I first saw her she was coming towards me from the other direction."

"But she asked for directions to Primrose Hill."

"No. She wanted to get to Chalk Farm tube station. From where she was then, Primrose Hill was the best route."

"So she'd overshot? She'd already passed the Primrose Hill exit so was retracing her steps?"

"If she had come from further down the canal, correct."

"Are you able to tell us where on the towpath you first met her?"

Patrick looked at Sanders. She put a neat full stop on the page and looked up. He thought quickly. James Mitchell had seen them together and after that the bloke came at them. Christ, he didn't know where to place this imaginary meeting.

"Um."

"Perhaps it would help to look at a map of the canal?"

"Yes it might. Thank you."

Sanders produced a map from the file in front of her.

The canal described a gradual arc from west to east through St John's Wood. Several bridges crossed it. Since he was making it up, Patrick could have placed the encounter anywhere. He shook his head.

"I'm sorry I just can't say. I was deep in thought, I remember that. I know the route so well I wasn't particularly taking in my surroundings."

Malek persisted.

"Well, let's try it from a different angle."

A line Patrick often used himself in court to herald danger.

"The woman stopped you and you offered to accompany her to Primrose Hill?"

"No, she asked for directions to Chalk Farm and I offered to accompany her as far as Primrose Hill Bridge, if that is what it is called."

"Apologies. And on the way you passed your colleague, Mr Mitchell."

"Yes."

"How long had you been walking with the woman before you passed Mr Mitchell?"

Good question.

"A minute or two. Maybe a little more. I'm sorry. I'm not being much help, but I don't want to mislead you."

"No of course not, sir. You are being very helpful. So you were not far from Primrose Hill?"

"Not far at all."

He looked back down at the map. He indicated locations with his index finger as he spoke.

"I mean from where I got onto the canal at this bridge here, which is it, No. 8, is it? Yes. From here to the bridge at the Primrose Hill exit, No. 10, right? There's this bridge in the middle, Bridge No. 9. I can't remember which side of this middle bridge I was on when saw James Mitchell but it was somewhere around there."

He drew a wide, rough circle around Bridge No. 9.

Malek smiled.

"She really was lost then, wasn't she?"

Patrick gave him a severe look. He had lost the mood for flippancy.

"She was lost, yes. Hence the need to ask for directions, no doubt. It was only a minute or so before we bumped into James Mitchell. I'm afraid I was not aware of the time."

He caught a look from Malek who then looked to his colleague. She leafed through the file again and brought out the photograph of Davey that she had shown to Patrick the previous evening.

"Just to remind you of the appearance of the deceased, sir."

Sanders pushed the photograph across the table towards Patrick. There was no doubt whatsoever in his mind that it was the man who had attacked him on the canal path.

Malek continued.

"This is Mr McBrain. Tests have confirmed that he did indeed drown. He also suffered the injuries I mentioned to you last evening. Did you see him at all, Mr Kingdom, during your walk?"

Another good question. Patrick stuck to his story.

"I honestly don't know. If I did, he did not register. As I say, I was thinking about work most of the way. I really was not interested in the people I passed. Where was his body found?"

Malek pointed to a spot between Bridge No. 9 and Primrose Hill Bridge. "Here. You may remember passing a short section of wall which is quite heavily graffitied. His body was recovered just there."

Patrick pulled on his left earlobe in thought. It was a signature mannerism. "I'm just thinking."

"Yes sir?" Malek asked.

"No, I'm just thinking that since the canal doesn't have a current, as a river does, then the deceased probably entered it quite close to where his body was found. Since neither Mr Mitchell nor I saw anything unusual on the path, then whatever caused the deceased to be in the canal must have occurred some time around or soon after seven o'clock, unless of course he was already under water when we passed, I suppose, but that doesn't seem very likely. Apart from anything else we were not the only people on the path. You would think someone would have seen him. And the injuries," he wafted his hand vaguely towards Sanders' file, "may be quite unconnected with his death. Would you agree?"

"We will consider all the evidence and form our conclusions, sir."

Patrick drew his feet beneath him and put his hands on his knees, ready to stand and leave.

"Indeed. Well, I'm not sure I can help you anymore, can I? Unless there's anything else?"

Malek looked at his notes thoughtfully.

"Can you explain why you took the main road home, sir, rather than go back along the path?"

Patrick looked at him directly. "I enjoy walking round in circles, detective constable."

Malek thanked Patrick, and after further courtesies wished him a happy Easter holiday. Sanders accompanied him back to the front desk. The whole interview had taken less than thirty minutes.

Patrick had lain awake all night agonising over it.

Every instinct had impelled him to volunteer the truth as soon as possible. Was he a suspect? He had not been cautioned, so presumably not. But if he left it too long to change his story and tell them what had really happened, they would naturally suspect him of concealing incriminating truths. He longed to describe the attack, to assure the police that he had merely defended himself and Gracia with only reasonable, lawful force. He would apologise for not having said all this sooner but could explain that he had not done so because he had not connected his attack with a man being found dead. A weak excuse, but just about plausible, he thought. By dawn that was the course he had decided to take. He had just needed Gracia to come clean too, to corroborate his account. Her flat refusal to back him up had given him no choice but to stick to his original story.

He breathed in deeply once more then began walking away from the station entrance. On balance, the interview had gone reasonably well but he was uneasy. Malek's tone of voice, added to Sanders' occasional eyebrow raises, had unnerved him. The consequences for him, should the police discover evidence that proved he had lied, would be catastrophic both professionally and personally.

Professionally he would be done for. No question. Disciplinary proceedings, disbarred, career over.

Personally, well. If it all went seriously tits up and he was charged with any kind of offence, whether connected with causing McBrain's death or for lying to the police, the chances were that his relationship with Gracia would come out. Jesus Christ! Jenny. Would she leave him? She might. All because of a fucking tramp.

He was walking towards the Euston Road. As he looked around for a cab he checked his thoughts, told himself that the police's concern was the man's death and that on that front his conscience was clear. He was not to blame. He had defended himself against a vicious and unprovoked assault.

The police did not need to know about it, nor who Gracia was. Noone else had witnessed it and she had made it perfectly clear that she had no intention of telling them she was even present. He need not worry.

When he turned onto the main road, cars and vans filed slowly past him, nose to tail in inch by inch progress. The illuminated orange light of a taxi emerged at a distance. He raised his arm. The cab pulled over and the window opened. He asked to be driven to Euston Station. The driver nodded. Patrick's spirits lifted. He got in and relaxed into the ample passenger space, comforted further by the prospect of a restful weekend at home.

"There's a bit of a hold up near the station, mate. Burst main I think," the driver warned him. "Catching a train?"

"Yes, but don't worry. I can always get the next one."

"Going anywhere nice?"

"Home for Easter." Patrick kept his sentence short. He was not in the mood for a chat.

"That'll be nice. Got kids have you?"

"Two boys."

"Nice. I could only do girls. My missis kept them after the divorce. Grown up now of course. But my partner, she's got boys. Thirteen and eleven. Right tearaways they are. Fun though."

Patrick decided the best way to close down the conversation was to say nothing at all.

He thought about his own sons.

His former boarding school had been favoured by three generations of Kingdom offspring. He had been a pupil there himself and had assumed that his own children would follow suit. He had been surprised to have to justify the point to Jenny.

"It'll make a man of him," he asserted as he looked into the baby-blue eyes of Rob, their first born, who lay cosily in his cot.

Jenny said that boarding school was not where she wanted her children to be educated, the staff at such institutions being paid employees, none of whom feels a parent's love for the children in their charge. She persuaded Patrick to wait at least until the boy was able to write his own name before making a decision. From an early age Rob showed signs of being bright, serious-minded and well-adjusted. Patrick recognised that there was every indication that he would grow into a rounded adult without the challenge of being torn from his parents' care during his formative years and he did not press the matter. Two years after Rob's birth Charlie burst in on the scene. His arrival was fast and late. His life followed suit. Here was a boy who fell into scrapes. The question of boarding came up again when Charlie was three and Rob well able to write his own name.

"It'll calm Charlie down, Jenny," argued Patrick as the boy splashed around in a puddle in dungarees and yellow wellies while his older brother looked on admiringly.

"It'll teach him to learn what's what in life. And Rob could do with toughening up a bit."

Jenny rarely met Patrick head-on in an argument but the moment had come.

"No, Patrick."

Patrick was taken aback by her directness. She continued.

"I didn't go to the trouble of giving birth to these children only for the reward of having them moulded into adults by someone else. Please don't let us talk about this again."

And Patrick recognised that for once he was beaten.

The boys attended a local private school where each of them excelled. Rob was made Head Boy, Charlie, Captain of Rugby. Both attended Exeter University (Rob – History, Charlie – Exercise and Sports Science). Rob was now twenty-seven and doing nicely in re-insurance. Last year he had purchased his first house, a Victorian terrace in Plaistow, East London.

Charlie had gone in on the bottom rung of an estate agency which had an office in Stratford. The boys got on well and it made perfect sense to them both for Charlie to rent Rob's second bedroom.

By the time the boys had established themselves in London, Patrick's work pattern had become more predictable. The ill-prepared brief delivered at 5:00pm for a half-day trial listed at short notice the following day was the bread and butter of more junior barristers. Seniority and bigger cases which were habitually listed to commence on a date well in the future demanded of Patrick more hours of work but greater flexibility over when it could be done. He had hoped that this might enable him to spend evenings with the boys at the theatre or for dinner. But it had not worked out that way. Rob was still relatively junior in his firm and was expected to impress his seniors by working late, so his free evenings were rare. Charlie had his own busy social life. So the dinners had been few and far between. It would be good to have the holiday weekend with them.

"Married, are you?"

The taxi driver's voice cut into his thoughts.

"Yes. Thirty years next year." He regretted giving the driver fuel for further enquiry.

"Thirty years." The driver had run his hand over his head in wonder. He chattered on about his own marriage and why it had failed. "Don't get me wrong, she was a lovely girl."

Patrick's mind returned to the New Year's Eve party in Oxford at which he had first met Jenny. He was twenty-one, she twenty-four. They were seated around a large table. Patrick was newly qualified and already showing early signs of talent as a junior barrister on the Midland and Oxford Circuit. On his left was a female archaeologist from St Anne's who had bloodshot eyes and a passion for Byzantine art. He turned to Jenny, seated on his right. Her other neighbour was talking animatedly to the man seated opposite him.

"So, you work for? Sorry, who did you say?" he asked.

Jenny smiled. She was pretty and fair haired. Her smile revealed that one front tooth slightly overlapped the other. It was a charming imperfection.

"Savill's? The property agents? I'm on their residential side. Sorry, that doesn't sound very interesting does it?"

"No, it does. How wonderful. So can you describe your dream home?" Jenny looked down, apparently hesitant, but stepped up to the challenge. "Well not exactly, but I think I know what I like."

"I bet you do," he replied, smiling also. "Go on."

And she began to describe the house they now lived in. "In the country." He agreed that country living was essential.

"Period."

"Excuse me? Do you need to leave the table?"

She hooted with laughter. "Sorry, jargon. I mean old. Maybe eighteenth century."

"Right."

"Big rooms, high ceilings, a kitchen everyone can sit in. Space outside for dogs maybe."

"Dogs?" He sounded doubtful.

"Definitely dogs. Don't you, I mean do you like them?"

"Oh very much. I intend to own several one day."

"Really? What kind?"

"I can't make up my mind. Just not Labradors."

Jenny put down her knife and fork. "Why not? Everyone loves Labradors."

Patrick laughed. "Well that's the problem. Don't you think they're a bit common?"

She laughed again. She really was enchanting. Patrick did not want her to turn back to her neighbour.

He continued. "So, go on. What else?"

Once again she took the bait.

"Oh, I don't know. What about a games room?"

Patrick looked quizzical. "Games? What are we talking, snooker, ping pong, deck quoits, indoor curling?"

She looked away. Blast. He should not have made fun of her so soon. "I suppose," he continued and then paused on the brink of a risk. She looked back.

"I suppose you might want to decorate the bedrooms with children one day. It sounds like that kind of house."

"Oh, absolutely," she replied. "Ten or twelve at least. And of course they would all have to be girls. I do like girls, you see."

Patrick was highly amused and delighted that she had introduced an element of nonsense into his fantasy world.

"Well, Jenny, twelve daughters could be hard to arrange. I'm more of a one-woman man, me. If it got into double figures, I think I could take fright. Maybe we should discuss this further one day, if you would like to?"

Their host's voice interrupted them. "You two! Jenny! Patrick! Stop talking and eat up. Everyone's ready for pudding and we have to finish eating before Big Ben!"

In the background, the taxi driver had moved on to how he had met his current partner while he was still married to his wife. For a while things appeared to have been a little messy, he having kept both women on the go.

"You never been tempted, squire?"

Patrick looked out of the window. The traffic had not moved for about five minutes. He considered getting out and walking the rest of the way, but as he formed the words to say so, the cars in front began to edge forward.

Tempted? Was that what it was? The word lacked sufficient substance to describe the intensity of his relationship with Gracia. To reduce it to a temptation made it sound like a fling but it had felt more than that. Either way, he considered, as he angled his head to try to see if the taxi was making merely temporary progress or whether the journey might end quite soon, either way, it was over and in some ways that was a relief.

He had recently heard a colleague describe his girlfriend as high maintenance. Yes, that was Gracia. It did not feel right to consider the women in his life by reference to their demands but, by comparison, Jenny could barely have been lower maintenance. He had never liked to dwell on which of the two women he would forsake if he were forced to choose. He had counted on it never coming to that. Both women satisfied him in a different way. Gracia presented excitement which fitted the rush and adrenalin of London life and work. But Jenny provided a stability which blended in with the peace and tranquility of home life. Gracia challenged him. Jenny accepted him. The thrills and unpredictability of his relationship with Gracia filled gaps that a wife of thirty years could not realise existed but, he asked himself, were thrills and unpredictability substantial qualities in a relationship? Of course they were not. Gracia had tantalised him. But maybe his driver had picked the right word after all. Maybe Gracia was merely a temptation to which he had fallen prey. He resolved to mend his ways. Jenny deserved better than a cheating husband. It was time to give her more attention. He would buy her some flowers at Euston. If he had to wait for a train, he would browse one or two of the shops, for something a bit nicer. A Moleskine perhaps. Or was there still an underwear shop at Euston? No, maybe the Moleskine.

He took his phone from his pocket and turned it on to ring Jenny to tell her which train he would be on. The display lit up with a list of missed calls, all from her. At least a dozen since the morning. He dialled and she answered immediately.

"Where've you been? I've been ringing for ages." She sounded frantic.

"Jenny, I'm so sorry. My phone's been off. What's the matter?"

"It's the boys." The words were clipped, her voice constricted. "They've had a car accident. They were on their way home. I don't know exactly what happened. Charlie was driving. He's hurt, but okay. But they're worried about Rob. It's really serious. We are at the John Radcliffe in Oxford. Where are you? Can you get here?"

Patrick spoke before his brain could process fully what she had said. "Yes of course. I'm still in London but I'll get there as soon as I can."

Her voice trembled.

"I think it's touch and go, Patrick."

He leant forward to the driver. "Sorry, can you take me to Marylebone instead?" They were on the Euston Road. The driver cheerfully agreed, glad of the extra mileage. Patrick checked the app on his phone to see which train he could catch. Then the phone rang again and Gray's name appeared on the screen.

"Gray, hello."

"Patrick, old chap. I thought we should have a catch up." He spoke in the easy, urbane manner that endeared him to all he met.

Patrick cut him short. Gray was deeply sympathetic, hoped to goodness that the boy would be OK and insisted that Patrick ring him if he needed to. Patrick agreed and rang off.

REGENT'S CANAL

4:30pm

Jalal found a place to park near Primrose Hill. He reached his left arm over to the back seat for his waterproof and grabbed the bundle of photographs from the passenger seat beside him. As an afterthought he took a bite of energy bar and washed it down with chocolate milk, justifying the snack to himself with uncertainty over how long this exercise would take. It wasn't that he believed himself to be unduly overweight, but he did know that his ample physique demanded that he really ought to avoid eating between meals.

He took the path that bounded Primrose Hill and crossed over Prince Albert Road onto the canal path, then struck west towards Bridge No 9. First he checked that the witness appeal sign was still in place and that no-one had messed with the writing. It was unbelievable, really, how often police notices were vandalised. Then he followed the path as far as Lisson Grove, which was the nearest he could get to Little Venice before having to divert onto pavements, turned round and retraced his steps back. This time he stopped at Bridge No. 9.

The sheltered areas under the side arches were populated by the usual types, most of them apparently sleeping. He approached a mound of cardboard and fabric. "Hello." He said. No reply. He raised his voice. "Excuse me." Still nothing. No movement. He could not even be sure that there was life within the makeshift cocoon, so he went higher up into the arch and tried another pile of ragged blankets, to similar effect. Further along was another shabby heap of bedding. "Hello?" he ventured. Dirty, gnawed fingertips emerged from within the grimy sheath of padding, hooking around the top edge to reveal a woman's face. In an Irish accent she told him to piss off. He crouched down beside her. She asked if he'd heard her and told him to piss off again. Jalal apologised and asked her to look at a criminal records photograph of David McBrain. He said that he was making enquiries into Mr McBrain's death which had occurred nearby between April 4th and 5th. She looked at the photograph, turned over and lay with her back to him.

Jalal slid back down the slope and looked around. There was no-one else to question and frankly he had had enough. He wished he was back in the office. Jayne could do this next time.

ISLINGTON POLICE STATION

4:30pm

Resentment was not a feeling Jayne enjoyed but how come she was the one who had copped her present task?

What did they have? A rough sleeper dead in the canal with spice and alcohol in his blood and injuries to his wrist and head along with a few other cuts and bruises. But look at nine out of ten of the people who sleep near the canal and you'll find the same. Only most of them don't end up in it. Miracle really.

Between them, she and Jalal had to view all the CCTV footage taken from every camera in the area from 2:00pm onwards on 4th April, the day before McBrain's body had been found. She knew it was necessary but of all the jobs in all the world, trawling through CCTV footage had to be the worst. This was far more Jalal's kind of thing but the lucky bastard was down at the canal again. She had already dredged through the footage from a camera above the bridge by the zoo which had been put up a few years ago after a spate of stone throwing at the warthogs. For warthog watching it had been riveting; sod all else.

Now she was back to footage from the camera near the crossing. The frames were grainy and drearily slow. She leant back in her chair, stretched, checked the time and rubbed her eyes, then re-focused. What time was she up to? 5:35pm. She doodled on her pad as she complained to herself about having had to go back so early in the day. OK, maybe to see if McBrain was around at any time. But even if he was, so what? That barrister had been right, nothing can have happened till after 7:00pm. Still, not too long to go now.

She looked back to the screen, clicked play and watched the comings and goings on the bridge. Suddenly she leant forward abruptly and stopped the recording. Went back and played it again. Three times.

"Busted!"

She lifted her phone and dialled Jalal.

"Jal, it's Jayne. The woman Kingdom met on the canal? The one he said was lost? She can't have been lost. She had only walked onto the canal from the same crossing an hour and twenty minutes earlier. Black bob, dark jacket, skirt, boots. Definitely her. What the fuck?"

EASTER SATURDAY 20th APRIL

WEST HADDON

7:00am

Shortly before midnight, Patrick had driven home from the hospital with Charlie, the younger, luckier brother who had been discharged with a broken collar bone, bruises and cuts. Jenny had stayed as close as possible to his elder brother.

Rob had been the passenger in the brothers' shared Ford Focus. His side of the car had taken the full impact of the motorbike travelling on the A-road outside Northampton which hit them head on when Charlie drove into its path from a side road. Rob's hip and pelvis were shattered. Severe abdominal bleeding from the liver had required urgent surgery which had lasted several hours. When it concluded, Rob was taken to the Intensive Care Unit where he was ventilated and placed in an induced coma. Late in the afternoon the surgeon, Mr Al-Shataar, had explained that management of internal bleeding was the current issue. Rob would be monitored carefully. They had to understand that his life was in danger and that the next forty-eight hours were critical.

Abstractedly, Patrick poured food in two dog bowls and placed them on the floor. Billy and Bunter greedily fell to slobbery chomplng as he stood up to make himself a cup of coffee. He had told Jenny to ring him if there was any news. She hadn't rung. He couldn't bear to wait any longer and dialled her number.

"Darling, how is he?"

Jenny's voice was flat. "Still the same. No change. I've sat with him most of the time but obviously he doesn't know I'm there." She lost control. "I feel so useless."

Patrick looked around. He had no idea how to comfort his wife. How in all honesty could he tell her that Rob was going to be OK? From his distorted perspective of involvement in murder trials, victims with the kind of injury his son had suffered never ended up being OK.

"I know, love."

"How's Charlie?" Her voice brightened a little.

"Still asleep. We spoke a bit last night."

It was too painful.

"He cried, Jenny. I haven't known him do that since he was a little boy." He shouldn't have told her.

Jenny took a breath. "Tell him it wasn't his fault."

"How can I? He knows it was. He said they'd been up late and decided to power through, that's how he put it. They thought it made sense to drive straight home to miss the traffic. He hadn't had a drink but he admits he was getting tired and just wanted to get home. He went straight over the junction. Never saw the bike coming at all. Never even saw the junction. Do you know how the driver is?"

"You have to look after him, Patrick. It's just, just too much. Tell him we're on his side. Tell him that his brother is going to be OK. No, I don't know about the chap on the bike. Oh God. Why didn't they go to bed?"

"I know, love. But we have to deal with this. Charlie is OK and Rob's in the best hands."

"I'll ring as soon as I know anything." Jenny sounded exhausted. "Have we done something to deserve this, Patrick? Have we?"

He looked down at his feet.

"Of course not. Did you get any sleep?"

"Not really. Will you come?"

"Of course. I'll wait till Charlie wakes up. He might be in shock. He might want to come too. I don't know. I'll text. Let me know if you hear anything."

"Course. Bye."

MANCHESTER SQUARE, MARYLEBONE

9:30am

That familiar moment of waking up with no idea of whereabouts as, one by one, the things that matter remind the conscious self that they are still there. Light from the gap in the curtains told Gracia that the day had begun. It was Easter Saturday. Throughout her childhood it had been a day of waiting just one more day to receive a huge chocolate egg. When she was little, her mother used to put a small creme egg beside her breakfast place with a note. "Just to make the time pass quicker." And Gracia would gobble it in one mouthful and coat her metal braces in chocolate and sugary gunk. Gray had continued the tradition throughout her teens. His note would say. "Just to hasten the day." Some years she left the egg there all day.

Her phone rang. Claudio. She gave in and answered.

"I've got nothing to say to you."

"Gracia, listen to me, please cara Gracia, per favore."

The Italian endearment 'cara' had enchanted Gracia so much more than its English translation 'dear' when they first met. Claudio's lingering emphasis on the first 'a' was as arousing to Gracia as a lover's touch and he knew that. His pronunciation of her name, shortening the 'a' and modulating the 'c' into a 'ch', to rhyme with focaccia, had amused her. This time his tone struck her as grovelling and despicable. She sighed.

"Go on then."

"Is not true, Gracia."

"Oh come on, Claudio. I've seen the photos."

He pleaded. She could imagine his hands gesticulating innocence. "No, veramente, is not true. Yes, I went in a club. I drank, I danced. I spoke to my friends. I spoke to their friends. I drank a lot, Gracia. I was stupid."

"I fucking know that."

"But no, it is not what the papers said. I was drunk and I boasted about you. I told them "My wife is Annie, you know? They all go "Wow, really!" In Italy *Initiate* is huge. They love you. One of the girls, she went to the papers with this photograph and story about a sex party. She will have been paid a lot of money. They don't care if it's true. I don't even know her name. The picture, you've seen the picture, right? We shared a cab. We were laughing and joking. I didn't know she had taken it. There were lots of us. There was no party. I went home alone Gracia, I swear to you."

The impossibility of not knowing whether this was true or just a good story clouded her mind as if she were feeling her way through fog.

"I swear it, Gracia."

She spoke slowly.

"Claudio. It doesn't matter whether or not it's true. Don't you see? By even saying my name you were taking a risk. Couldn't you, just for once, have shut the fuck up?"

"Carissima I am so sorry. I know. Sono stupido. What can I do? Shall I go to the paper too? Tell them is a lie?"

"For God's sake, Claudio, no. Don't go anywhere near a newspaper. It just drags out the story. If they come to you then, I don't know, say it is not true and you have nothing to add. Nothing, do you get it?"

"I am so sorry, Gracia. Forgive me?"

"I don't know. I'm tired."

She threw the phone to the end of the bed and curled up in a ball.

At midday she woke again. She had slept more lightly this time and knew exactly where she was. Into her mind came the first time she had come home from school after Gray had completed the alterations to the upstairs flat which resulted in her new bedroom. She was thirteen. Gray had prepared her during the drive.

"You'll see your new room," he had announced. His voice sounded artificially upbeat and nervous.

Her childhood bedroom in Clapham had been brightly decorated in vibrant yellows and greens chosen before her birth to allow for the possibility of her being either a boy or a girl. Every birthday her mother had hand painted a little red parrot with an orange beak somewhere in the room, on a skirting board perhaps, or at the junction between wall and ceiling, or above the bookshelf. As a child, Gracia had loved the excitement of the treasure hunt for each newly painted parrot. Just one more little ritual lost when the helicopter ditched into the sea.

Gray had continued, "I wasn't sure about the colour scheme so I asked Vanessa what she thought."

It had seemed that, by giving the new decor in her bedroom the stamp of his girlfriend's approval, Gray had imagined that it might add to its appeal.

"And what did Vanessa decide I would like my new room to be like?"

"You'll see. Don't worry though. It's nothing too radical. Just maybe not as babyish as before but, hopefully, something that you'll like over the years, as fashions change and as you go on and off things."

Gracia could tell that Gray was quoting the interloper he had co-opted to psycho-analyse her future taste.

When they got home she was encouraged to go upstairs on her own to look.

The walls were primrose yellow. At the window hung pretty curtains of narrow, pale green and cream stripes set behind printed posies. Gracia looked around the room in horror. It was mimicry, a pathetic pastiche, some kind of attempt by Vanessa to match Gracia's mother's colour scheme. But it was nowhere near. The colours and patterns were all wrong, the gentle tones no more than a sarcastic reminder of all that she had lost. No parrots.

She burst into tears of rage. Why had Gray not asked her what she wanted? How dare he presume that Vanessa would know better? Why had he elected to please Vanessa over pleasing her?

She pulled her pencil case from her bag, wrenched the zip aside and took the compass from her geometry set.

At the bottom of the stairs Gray was smiling affectionately. "We didn't want it to be too different, but perhaps just a bit more grown up? I hope you like it. The bedside table belonged to your granny."

Gracia burst into tears once more. Gray asked her again and again what was the matter? What had he done wrong? She despised him for not knowing.

A breath of wind blew across her face. Her mind returned to the present and she opened her eyes. A pretty posie confronted her.

She sat up and turned the bedside table sideways in order to see the back. 'Fuck you, Gray.' had been dug furiously into the wood in childish writing.

She righted the table and pushed it firmly back against the wall.

On the kitchen table, a creme egg lay on a plate beside the usual note. Gray was pouring coffee beans into a grinder. The Saturday Telegraph lay on the worktop. He must have been out already. He turned round and smiled.

"Sleep OK?"

She picked up the egg and, without removing her eyes from him, unwrapped it as she walked towards him, then stopped, stood still and put it into her mouth, whole.

"Thank you so much." came out as a honking gabble. Chocolatey dribble oozed from her mouth and down her chin. Tears of laughter streamed down her cheeks. She tore a piece of kitchen paper from the roll and wiped her mouth, then hugged him for the first time in many years, laughing still, then crying. He hugged her back.

ANGEL

9:30am

Disappointing, no infuriating, that was what Jalal's response had been yesterday evening. Jayne thought he would have rushed straight to the station there and then to see with his own eyes that the woman on the crossing with Patrick Kingdom had been in that exact place only an hour and twenty minutes earlier. But no. All he'd done was tell her to log it and keep going. He'd have a look in the morning. Jayne could not believe it. Sometimes she couldn't decide if Jalal was thick or lazy or both.

Dressed in pyjama bottoms, T-shirt and fluffy yellow flip-flops, she walked lazily from her bedroom to the kitchen, yawning. Her sister was leaning against the work surface spooning cereal into her mouth from a large mug. "Hey Caz." Jayne put her hand on the eighteen-year old's shoulder.

"Hey. No work?"

"Late start. No netball?"

"Holiday."

"Where's mum?"

"Work."

Meaning Sainsbury's.

"Dad?"

"Same."

Black cab driver.

Jayne selected her favourite mug from the cupboard and put the kettle on. As it crackled and steamed to the boil she asked, "What are you doing today?"

"Absolutely nothing." Caz stretched the words to their limit as she walked over to the sink with her mug. For a moment it looked like she might wash it up, but instead she left it on the drainer and went into the sitting room to flump down onto the sofa to scroll through her phone.

"Hey. Come and look at this."

Jayne pressed her teabag against the side of the mug and flicked it out into the bin with a teaspoon.

"Coming."

"Sit here." Caz indicated the cushion next to her. "Who's this?"

Caz loved games. It didn't matter to her if it was netball or a quiz. She held out her phone to show Jayne the *Mail Online Showbiz* page, covering the text with her thumb.

Jayne looked at the picture then back at her sister.

"Go on." Caz could barely contain her excitement at the prospect of Jayne guessing wrong.

Jayne looked at the image of a smartly dressed young woman apparently walking past a restaurant. She was wearing a black jacket, tight jeans, boots, sunglasses, hair styled in a black bob. A black bob.

"Show me some more."

Caz did.

"Where is this?"

"Chiltern Firehouse apparently. Come on."

"Give me the phone." Jayne took it from Caz's grip and scrolled back and forth. The headline read:

'Gracia Peel Goes Dark In Wake Of Husband's Sex Romp'.

She looked up at her sister's deflated expression. "Is that a wig?"

"No, spoilsport, she's dyed it. That's what it's saying, 'goes dark', get it? Give it back."

Jayne got up and left the room. Her sister's voice followed her. "Give me my phone back!"

She picked up her own phone from beside her bed to text Malek.

Hi, Jal. Meeting you at the station at 11, right? Got something really interesting to show you now. J.

LITTLE VENICE

10:00am

"Where is everyone?" Emily Mitchell, aged eighteen, strolled barefoot into the garden wearing little other than a blue and white striped rugby shirt belonging to Titchfield J, according to the outsized name tape above her left breast. James was reading the paper, seated at their pretty wrought iron table with a cup of freshly brewed coffee to hand. He had no idea who Titchfield J was, nor how his daughter had come by his rugby shirt. 'He decided not to ask and answered, "Mum's at the shops. Jake and Eve are in bed. Whose is that shirt?"

Hadn't meant to do that.

Emily underlined the name tape with her right forefinger and raised her eyes meaningfully. "Take a guess, Dad."

Conversation over, she turned and sashayed back into the kitchen.

James returned to *The Times Review* section. He felt like a good read over the holiday and turned the pages to the bestsellers list.

"Think I'll go to Waterstones later," he called through. "Want to come?"

Either Emily hadn't heard or did not regard his question as sufficiently interesting to deserve a reply. For whatever reason, she didn't answer. He didn't push it.

"Look at you!" Emily's voice, raised and mocking, distracted him from his reading and he went inside to see what was going on. Sixteen-year-old Eve, blonde hair dragged back into a ponytail, was bouncing on a pair of pink running shoes. Lycra leggings and vest, both pink, stretched around her body. Kicking her feet high behind her, she sprang to the kitchen sink and turned on the tap.

"Going for a run?" asked James, sitting himself down at the table.

"No, ice skating actually, Dad." She rolled her eyes at Emily who giggled, put her chin in her hand, elbow on the table and leant over to him.

"Was it your powers of deduction or something else that made you know you'd make a good barrister, Dad?" She looked over to her sister. "He's buzzing this morning, Eve. He asked me whose shirt this is!"

The girls giggled some more, gently mocking their father. James didn't particularly mind being the butt of their jokes. It was the arguing that got him down. He saw plenty of conflict at work and although it was normally conducted in a well-regulated framework of good manners and decency, he had had enough of it by the time he got home. Once there, all he wished for was peace. With three bright, teenaged children in the household, that was a wish that was rarely granted.

"Hey, seen this?" Eve took her phone from the pocket stitched into the back of the waistband of her leggings and showed the screen to her sister. "You'd never believe it was Gracia Peel, would you?"

Emily reached out her hand. "Let's see?" She enlarged the screen. "Gosh, no you wouldn't actually. She looks so different. How did they even recognise her?"

"Do you think her hair's like that for a new film?"

"I don't know. I read somewhere that the second series of *Initiate* is about to be filmed. But Annie is blonde. So's Gracia, isn't she?"

"Totally, yeah. No, it's always blonde. Maybe Annie has to have a short black bob for a new storyline? So maybe the press know she's had to change her hair and were looking out for her so they could get the first pictures. Do you like it?"

"I don't know. Makes her look older."

"Let me see." James also had succumbed to the family addiction to *Initiate*. Gracia Peel was a beautiful actress. He hoped he would not be put off her by this new look. Eve handed him her phone and asked what he thought.

He bent forward to look closer.

"You don't have to get closer, Dad. You just enlarge the screen." Deftly, Eve did so. The image grew clearer, then more blurred. James took the phone from her.

"Let me look. I know what to do."

"OK, chill."

James swiped through the ten pictures of Gracia, black-bobbed and stern-faced outside the Chiltern Firehouse.

"Are you sure that's Gracia Peel? Shame she's wearing sunglasses."

Eve pointed to the text.

"Says it is, doesn't it. Neeugh Dad, you can stop perving over her now. Give me my phone back?"

"What did you say?" asked James.

"I said stop perving over Gracia Peel."

"No, before."

"I didn't say anything before."

"You made a noise, a kind of yeuching noise."

Eve looked at her father with mock sympathy. "It's the noise Annie makes in *Initiate*. Everyone does it. It's a thing."

The front door opened then slammed and Carrie came in, bearing bagfuls of shopping for an Easter Sunday lunchtime feast. Eve greeted her.

"Hey Mum. Good that you're back. Dad's having a mental breakdown."

JOHN RADCLIFFE HOSPITAL, OXFORD

10:00am

Charlie had woken up looking bruised and shattered. He said he was fine and of course they had to go to the hospital. They had brought food for Jenny. She could not eat. The three of them sat together in the relatives' room. No one had anything to say.

ISLINGTON POLICE STATION

11:00am

Two TV monitors stood on the table before Jalal. To his left was a split screen showing frozen CCTV images of the woman on the crossing on April 4th. The left-hand image showed her at 6:00pm crossing from Primrose Hill towards the canal. The right-hand image appeared to show the same woman on the same crossing walking in the opposite direction away from Patrick Kingdom towards Primrose Hill one hour and twenty minutes later. The second monitor displayed the previous Thursday's *Mail Online* images of Gracia Peel outside the Chiltern Firehouse. His eyes flicked to and fro.

Jayne spoke with triumphant certainty. "See what I mean?"

Jalal leant forward, thinking aloud. "The hair's the same. The boots could be the same. Ditto the jacket. But loads of women have short dark hair, and wear jackets and long boots."

He leant back, causing the plastic chair in the interview room to bend and creak beneath the strain. He grimaced. He just wasn't sure.

"OK, let's take it a step at a time." Jayne's tone was emphatically patient. "Do we at least agree that these two women are the same person?" She pointed from one side of the left-hand screen to the other with her pen.

Jalal was not willing to be rushed. He looked carefully, narrowing his eyes. Even though the left-hand image showed the woman from the front and the right-hand image from behind her, yes, OK, exactly the same clothing and hair, same woman on the bridge at 6:00pm and 7:20pm.

Jayne pulled her chair in. She obviously felt she was getting somewhere. With that one movement she could not have expressed more eloquently that what she was demonstrating was blindingly obvious and the only obstacle to progress being made in the case was his inability to see it.

But, he was sorry, it was not that obvious to him, and he wasn't willing to pretend otherwise.

"And is it the same woman outside the Chiltern Firehouse?" she laboured, stabbing at the right-hand screen. Then she leant back, folding her arms and looked into her lap as Jalal struggled, looking from one screen to the other, brow creased with doubt.

"I don't know Jayne. She's wearing different clothes. The angles are different. And she's got sunglasses on."

Jayne unfolded her arms and sighed.

"OK, forget the clothes. Look at the way she walks." She jabbed her biro at each screen in turn. "Here when she's going to Primrose Hill, here when she's coming back and here when she's gone past the restaurant. The left arm is really far forward. And look at the angle of her body. It's identical. Jal, please, I spent the whole bloody afternoon looking at this footage yesterday. I know it's her."

He cupped his chin in his fist, elbow resting on the table, and shook his head. "It's difficult."

Jayne sighed in exasperation.

He continued, "And what if it is her? Where does that get us?"

Jayne shook her head in disbelief and turned her face towards him, leaning into his personal space. "Are you joking?"

He ignored the sarcasm and pursued his train of thought.

"Just say we interview Gracia Peel and she says it wasn't her. We're stuffed then, aren't we?"

Jayne did not like to contemplate this possibility but had to admit that that would be annoying.

"Maybe." She put her pen down onto the table. "But at the very least, if the two women on the crossing are the same we have a few more questions for Mr Smoothy Pants Patrick Kingdom 'cos I don't know about you but I'm not sure I believe that guy. And it's got to be worth at least asking Gracia Peel the question, hasn't it?"

Her eyes flashed in excitement.

"I mean she's only one of the biggest names trending on Twitter at the moment. I can hang with that, can't you?"

Jalal looked at her, unmoved. He loathed her flippancy.

Jayne gripped his forearm. "Come ON, Jal. You know how much pressure we're under to get this sorted. If this all pays off Cartwright will be well impressed, and the DI."

Jalal sighed and succumbed to her energy. "Okay, do we check with Cartwright first that it's OK to interview her?"

Jayne shook her head. "After what he said last time? No way. He wants a result, not a running commentary."

Jalal was still hoping for a get-out. "How do we get hold of her? Ring her up? How do we get her number? That's not going to be easy."

Jayne opened a new tab on one of the screens, typed in Google then 'Gracia Peel agent'. The answer came up immediately. She copied the contact number into her phone, saying,

"Jeez Jal, did you get enough sleep last night?" Sometimes he really disliked his partner.

MANCHESTER SQUARE, MARYLEBONE

1:00pm

Over breakfast, Gray had watched Gracia scroll through the online images of herself outside the Chiltern Firehouse, cup of coffee in hand. He dreaded more tears and frustration but she had merely commented "Was always going to happen wasn't it."

She had gone upstairs to get dressed and came back down wearing a casual but expensive looking tracksuit. "I think I'll go to the Landmark for a swim. Can't be bothered to go all the way home to get my stuff. But pretty sure I'll be able to buy a costume somewhere. Are you in later? I could do supper, if you like?"

After she left, he texted Patrick. He urgently needed to speak to him. Rob, of course, was his main concern, but there was also the other matter. He worded his message carefully. First things first.

> Patrick. Don't reply if difficult but do let me know how things are. Thinking of you. Gray.

Five minutes later his phone announced a reply.

> Gray. Thank you. Charlie discharged. Broken collar bone. Rob shattered pelvis. Severe internal bleeding. Long operation. Currently ventilated in ICU. Induced coma. Prognosis uncertain. P.

THE LANDMARK HOTEL, MARYLEBONE

2:00pm

Claridge's boasts one of the finest curved staircases of any hotel in London. The Savoy is abundantly Art Deco and has a unique drive-round entrance. The Ritz takes overall beating but the Palm Court Piano Bar at the Landmark Hotel was one of Gracia's favourite places in the world, not least because she could expect to go there undisturbed since the paparazzi generally stalk hotels with a higher profile. To her the luxury of access without unwanted attention justified every penny of the annual Spa subscription.

She walked beneath the glass roof past lofty palms which framed the dining area where couples and families sat enjoying lunch. The atmosphere was unrushed and hospitable. The Spa was located on the lower floor.

In the changing room she put on the new white one-piece costume she'd found in a boutique on Marylebone High Street and checked herself in the mirror. Not bad. Then she gathered her phone and magazine and walked through to the pool. Here the lighting was subdued. Dark tiles surrounded the water which lay still and inviting.

She stood on the side and gingerly dipped one foot into the water, then swished it from side to side to test the temperature. Comfortably reassured, she stepped down to waist height, leant forward and pushed herself forward. Breaststroke to begin with, throwing her legs wide and frog-like, loving the feeling of kick, stretch and glide. Then she moved up a gear into front crawl. Her hands cut through the water then pulled it past her while her legs and feet motored behind. Length after length, ten then twenty, every sideways breath filling her lungs with air which then bubbled out underwater, again and again. At each end she touched the side, turned, curled, pushed off and glided, weightless, head down, arms stretched out in front and then powered forward again.

Only after fifty lengths did she stop, breathing heavily, climb out and walk back to flop down on the lounger. She picked up her phone. Two missed calls. One from an unknown number. The other from her agent. Odd, on a Saturday. He'd left a voicemail.

"Gracia, listen love, the Claudio story. The producers have been on the phone. They're not happy but I've told them it hardly reflects badly on you. They're happy to let it die down over Easter but are talking about putting out a statement some time next week maybe, I think they want to turn bad news into good news, you know, make use of it with a positive spin? I'll keep you posted. Anyway, in other news, I've had a policewoman on the phone. Don't worry I don't think you're in trouble. She said she wants to talk to you about something that happened on Regent's Canal a few weeks ago. I hope you don't mind but I gave her your number so she'll probably ring. It's bona fide. I checked. She gave me a number to call back and it's Islington Police Station. Anyway, thought I'd give you a heads up. Let's talk after the weekend, OK? Love you."

She put her phone down onto the tiled floor and turned onto her side.

ISLINGTON POLICE STATION

4:00pm

"How do I look?"

Jayne had taken a lot of trouble over her appearance. Standing in the dreary surroundings of an interview room, she stretched her arm out to lean on the table and affected a stylish pose, placing one hand behind her head. Jalal looked up.

"Fine?" The interrogatory inflection told her he couldn't have cared less.

"Fine." She returned to business. "I'll get her in, shall I? Just remember, she's here voluntarily. She's not under arrest."

ISLINGTON POLICE STATION

4:15pm

Rarely had Gracia felt so irritated. Her afternoon had been ruined. She had had to leave the Landmark, flog to Islington Police Station and then wait, for God's sake, while they got their act together. It wasn't as if she could have said no when they rang, however much they banged on about the fact that they would be grateful if she could attend merely to help with enquiries, though she could bring her solicitor with her if she wanted to. Fuck that. And now, seated before her were two low-ranking and apparently starstruck policemen (OK maybe only the woman was star-struck) playing her some shitty CCTV footage and asking if she was one of the people it purported to show because, to quote the over made-up half-wit "I might be wrong but there is a striking similarity between that woman and the one shown in the pictures outside the Chiltern Firehouse in the *Daily Mail* online, and that was you, wasn't it?" JeSUS! She leant back in her chair and gave them her best press interview stare, the one she saved for really stupid questions.

"Thank you for inviting me here. I will be as helpful as I can. First, yes, I can confirm that I was outside the Chiltern Firehouse, as these photographs show, on Friday 19th April, yesterday in fact, just after seven o'clock in the evening. I was wearing a black wig, as I occasionally do as a disguise to avoid unwanted press attention. Sadly, on this occasion, it failed. As for this CCTV footage recorded on 4th April, all I can see are two indistinct figures on a crossing. One is male, you say. A Mr. Patrick Kingdom? Never heard of him. The other female. If that is so, I am not her. Neither am I the person in the footage taken of the same place earlier the same evening. I was at home that afternoon. In the evening I visited my former guardian, Sir Graham Andrew. You will find him during the day at the Royal Courts of Justice. He is a High Court judge, so a busy man, as you'll imagine and I am sure that, like myself, would prefer to be troubled only if necessary. This interview, I might say, does not strike me as having been necessary since I know absolutely nothing about how a body ended up in a canal, and, to my knowledge, I have never seen this other person whose photograph you have shown me. So, all in all, I'd say we're done here, wouldn't you?"

She stood up, turned round and pushed her chair in neatly beneath the table, then walked slowly from the room without closing the door behind her. The female constable's voice followed her into the corridor.

"I thought she'd be nicer than that, didn't you?"

***

Gracia Peel's response had impressed Jalal. Clearly, they'd reached a dead end as far as this line of enquiry was concerned. He was about to say so as Jayne spoke.

"She was lying." Jayne shut the door and turned to him for a reaction. "Come on, Jal. The CCTV isn't that bad. We've agreed, haven't we, that the woman on the bridge with Kingdom was also there an hour and twenty minutes earlier. Gracia Peel has got the same boots as her, the same jacket and the same hair and just now Gracia Peel got really cross with us, which is what people always do when they're in a corner." She reached for the phone.

Jalal opened his hand in supplication then let it drop to the table. "Now what are you doing?"

"Ringing that barrister."

"Kingdom?"

"No the other one. James Mitchell, the one who rang in."

He didn't bother to ask why she didn't ring Kingdom straight away. He didn't fully understand why they hadn't rung him already. But he did know what Jayne was like when she had a theory. Sometimes it was easier to just let her do it her way.

LITTLE VENICE

5:05pm

Heaven. James Mitchell lay back on his all-weather lounger. The sun was still warm, lunch over and washed up, the children flopped around the house doing he cared not what. Carrie had made her usual point that the loungers did not go with the Italianate effect of the garden but, after ten minutes of upright discomfort on a wrought iron chair, she had succumbed to the lure of a fabric covered cushion. She was dozing. He shut his eyes. Heaven.

His back pocket vibrated. Phone. Unknown number. Better take it. "Hello, James Mitchell here."

DC Sanders introduced herself. This sounded interesting. He sat up.

"Oh hello. How can I help?"

She explained that enquiries concerning the body found in the canal on April 5th were continuing and that they were following up some leads. She wondered if he might be able to assist with more detail about the woman he saw with Patrick Kingdom. James bridled. It seemed odd that they should be asking him.

"I'm not sure. I think I told you everything when I rang in."

Silence at the other end of the call invited him to continue.

"Have you spoken to Mr Kingdom? I think he's best placed to give a better description. I literally just jogged past them."

The constable confirmed that they had spoken to Mr Kingdom. She wondered if he could spare the time to go to the station to look at some photographs.

James stood up. Carrie lolled her head sideways to look questioningly at him.

"Sorry, I'm needed at Islington Police Station. Won't be long."

Thirty minutes later DC Sanders showed him the Chiltern Firehouse images that he had seen on Eve's phone earlier in the day, along with other stock images taken from the internet. Gracia's name was not shown.

"Gracia Peel?" he asked. Sanders nodded.

"Yes sir."

"I should say that I have already seen these images of her outside the restaurant. My daughter showed them to me this morning. She's rather an *Initiate* fan. Well, we all are actually." He collected himself. "You are asking if the woman I saw with Patrick Kingdom was Gracia Peel?"

"Yes sir."

Sanders touched the tip of her biro to the paper in front of her, making a tiny dot then revolved it, slid it through her thumb and forefinger and touched the same place with the other end, then repeated the movement as she and Malek waited for a reply.

James sat back. The chair made its usual complaint. He was not comfortable with the idea of discussing Patrick's companion.

"Surely Mr Kingdom is better placed to answer this than I am?

Sanders' expression did not alter. "We are pursuing that line of enquiry, sir." First principles – play it straight. He looked at Sanders, then Malek. "Look, I don't know if it was her or not. It could have been. It could well have been. The dark hair is the same though that's confusing because I've only ever seen her with fair hair. And if I'm honest I did wonder if she was someone I recognised when I saw her on the canal, though I couldn't place her then. Look, she bears a strong resemblance, put it like that."

He thought for a moment.

"There is one other thing though. Bit odd, but as we were talking she tripped on an uneven piece of brick from which part of the canal path is built and landed in a puddle. She made a noise. Sort of "Nyugh". It's exactly the same noise as her character sometimes makes in the Netflix series. My daughter does it too but it doesn't sound quite the same. The noise the woman on the canal made, I'd say was identical. Funny thing to remember I know, but sometimes I think actors reveal a bit of themselves when they make expressions, noises and stuff. It's like a sort of tic, do you know what I ..." He didn't finish the sentence.

Sanders' biro stopped moving. She looked up. "Neeugh."

"Yes, that's it."

Sanders looked to Malek. Something passed between them which James could not interpret. She spoke.

"Well, that is very helpful Mr Mitchell. Thank you very much. I'm sorry to have bothered you on a holiday weekend. Let me show you out."

He walked to his car. Should he ring Patrick? He was not sure he knew him well enough. Perhaps he should leave it for now.

MANCHESTER SQUARE, MARYLEBONE

7:00pm

From the snug, Gray heard the loud key turn, open and slam of the front door announcing Gracia's return. She made a noisy passage through the hall to the kitchen then shouted: "Gray!"

He put down the paper and went through. A supermarket bag lay on its side on the kitchen floor. Most of the contents had rolled or spilt out: wine, vegetables, prawns, chicken, raspberries, noodles, rice vinegar, garlic, sour cream, blinis, smoked salmon. She was on her knees, gathering things together and reaching up to put them on the worktop.

"I got us a feast. You won't believe what happened though. Drink? It's red. Or have you got one?" She picked up the bottle of wine and described her afternoon, colouring in the story with exaggeratedly unflattering descriptions of the two detectives and their dismal workplace as she assembled two glasses.

"The CCTV was really crap, Gray. It could have been anyone. No way was I going to say it was me with Patrick. So I just told them that I was here with you all evening. Because we said, didn't we? They'll leave it at that now I'm sure. Here." She handed him a well-filled glass of Beaujolais. "Shall I start to cook?" Then she looked at him. "What's up?"

Gray had been agitated ever since receiving Patrick's message earlier on. He desperately wanted to know if Rob's condition had improved. Should he tell Gracia about the accident? Perhaps Patrick would rather tell her himself, or prefer that she did not know at all. Unable to settle to any focused activity he had gone out for a walk around the lake in Regent's Park. By the time Gracia returned he had decided to tell her. Conceivably she might want to contact Patrick, at least pass on a message of concern. Even if she wanted to do nothing, she should at least know. His mind settled, he had sat down to read the paper.

Now this bombshell. It took him several moments to absorb the impact of her news. She had lied to the police and given him as her alibi in an investigation into an unexplained death. She evidently thought everything about that was absolutely fine and was ready to serve up a feast. He felt himself to be completely out of control. Gracia took a mouthful of wine and swallowed.

"What's the matter?" she asked.

Did she not understand?

He placed his glass on the worktop and took a breath. Tell her about Rob first. Then think what to do about her interview with the police.

"Gracia, I've got some bad news."

She listened as he told her what he knew about Rob's accident. Her eyes grew wide in shock then a furrow of concern embedded itself between them.

"Is he going to be OK?"

"I don't think they know."

Her hand covered her mouth. "How dreadful."

"I thought I might text Patrick again and ask how he is. I don't want to trouble him but I could say I'm thinking of him." Gray looked to her for consensus.

"Do that."

"Do you want me to tell him that you're here too and he's in both our thoughts?"

"No."

She started to leave the room then turned. "Surely the police will leave him alone about the canal thing, now he's got all this going on?"

Gray needed time to think.

"We'll talk about it later. I'll put this stuff away. Is there anything I can do about the cooking?"

Abstractedly, she looked at the mess on the floor. "No, it's fine. I'll deal with it in a bit. I'm going upstairs."

Gray returned to the snug. He lifted his phone. Holding it in one hand he tapped out a message to Patrick with one finger.

P. Thinking of you all. Here to talk if you need me. G.

LITTLE VENICE

8:00pm

The children were bickering over whose turn it was to clear away the dishes but, instead of playing his usual role of referee, James stood aside reflecting on his visit to Islington. All he could deduce from the fact that the police had asked him about Gracia Peel was that Patrick had not known who she was. Odd that, because he had had the impression that they were acquainted. Oh well. Ha! Patrick might be amused to discover that unwittingly he could have been in the company of a famous actress. Should he phone him? No. Still too much of an intrusion. Email? Possibly, but Patrick might not see it until after the holiday. Send a text? No, over friendly. Email him. Yes, no rush, after all. He went into his study.

Canal Enquiries

<James.Mitchell@yahoo.co.uk>
To: Patrick Kingdom

Patrick
Islington police called me in today to comment on a theory they are pursuing that the woman we both saw on the canal on April 4th might have been Gracia Peel (famous actress – see attached!!!!) I think they could be right. Not 100% sure. Thought you'd be amused!
Best
James

He attached a link to the Chiltern Firehouse story, clicked Send and returned to the kitchen. The girls were flicking soapy clouds at each other from a mountain of bubbles which was erupting from the sink. Then Jake went too far and scrunched a handful into Eve's hair. She whirled round and pressed too much of it into Jake's face, rubbing it around his nose. He gave her a push in the stomach and it clearly hurt. She stepped away and jabbed a martial arts kick at him with her right leg. It missed Jake but her foot connected with a glass on the kitchen table which smashed onto the floor. James looked at them and then at Carrie who stood helplessly by. "Get the dustpan and brush, someone," he said, and walked through to the twinkling peace of the garden.

WEST HADDON

11:00pm

Patrick sat with a glass of whisky staring at nothing, thinking nothing.

Rob remained in a critical condition. Periodically during the day Patrick had sat by his bed, sometimes with Jenny, sometimes alone. Rob had lain motionless and unresponsive, connected by needles and tubes to machines which breathed for him and monitored invisible functions. His eyes were closed. Patrick had longed to touch and stroke his face as he had done when Rob was a baby but had been restrained by fear of upsetting the precarious balance between life and death. Instead, he had searched his son's face for tiny indications of life while his mind had scanned the years during which Rob had grown from a cautious boy into a caring and careful adult who was generous to his younger brother and kept in touch with his parents. He was a good man.

During the afternoon Mr Al-Shaater had come to tell them that, provided Rob's condition did not deteriorate, a second operation would be carried out tomorrow to check the abdominal bleeding. All they could do was wait and hope.

By the evening, it was clear that Jenny and Charlie were struggling. She had had virtually no sleep since Thursday night. Charlie was in pain from his own injuries though clearly unwilling to admit the fact. They both needed to be at home. The ICU nurse had assured them that Rob would be under constant observation and promised to ring, if necessary. Jenny had still dithered, tied umbilically to the need to be with her wounded child.

Eventually Patrick had persuaded her to leave. At home they had eaten soup from the freezer and she and Charlie had gone straight to bed.

The glass slipped in Patrick's grip and he woke up. Automatically he checked his phone.

Messages. A kind one from Gray. He would ring him back in the morning. Emails. He scrolled through.

From: Mitchell J.

Subject: Canal Enquiries.

The whole saga returned to his mind. He read the email and closed his eyes but his brain would not rest. It darted around the people and present circumstances of his life forming visual images in his imagination as he desperately sought a peaceful resting place. Mentally, he felt ambushed from every side by the hostile forces of fear and chance.

Home should have been his safe place but his family was inseparable from his picture of home and Rob's life was hanging by a thread. Charlie appeared broken. Jenny was holding up but who knew what devastation to her shattered nerves lay ahead. There was no resting place for him here. His role was to be the father, the strong one. He wanted to weep.

He raised his glass to his lips as his mind's eye moved to London. His flat.

Evenings with Gracia, laughing, eating, playing, making love. But then he recalled the argument. Gracia had left him, or he had left her. Whichever. The break up had been more or less civil but had left a bad taste. No solace there.

Mentally he wandered, lost, searching desperately for peace. The large black door at the entrance to his Chambers welcomed him in. He had been happy there for nigh on thirty years. He imagined himself sitting at his desk, content for a moment or two. But then he looked around. Piles of boxes and files surrounded him, each one containing a complex maze of conflicting accounts of a serious crime which either prosecution or defence looked to him to present in favourable terms to a jury. Mentally he ran screaming from the pressure, straight into the arms of DCs Malek and Sanders. At any point they might telephone him.

The scene played out vividly in his head: "Mr Kingdom? We would like to ask you one or two more questions concerning your movements on the evening of April 4th. Would you to come down to the station, sir? It might be advisable to bring your lawyer."

Who had he been trying to kid when he thought they would never find out that he had lied to them? CCTV. They were on it already. James Mitchell's email told him that the police now suspected that Gracia was the woman he was with on the canal. Everything was closing in. He did not think there were cameras outside his mansion block but there could easily be one somewhere else around the neighbourhood which had caught him and Gracia walking side by side from his flat onto the canal path. Story blown.

"Tell me, Mr Kingdom, why did you lie about that?" He threw his head back and moaned, then lifted his legs to lie sidelong on the sofa, holding his head in both hands, eyes tight shut. One quiet word escaped his lips. "Help."

He must have slept. He dreamed of sitting with Gray in the snug at Manchester Square, surrounded by comfort and order. Gray. For a second or so he felt the warmth of solace engulf him. Gray represented safety, reason, understanding. He needed to talk to Gray. He checked his watch. It was 3:00am.

He stood up, poured another whisky, too large, put it on the side table next to the sofa and walked outside. The dogs looked up as he passed them. "All right, chaps. Not now. Go back to sleep, OK."

His shoes crunched on the gravel. He looked up at the stone mullioned windows. The main bedroom light was off. Was Jenny sleeping? He hoped so. Charlie's light was still on. What was the poor boy doing at this time of night? Pray God he had fallen asleep without turning off the light. Patrick smiled. That would be rather typical.

He stepped onto the grass which glistened with the beginnings of a dew and walked across the lawn to sit on a bench which looked over gentle countryside. Dark cloud hid the moon. The air was cold and fresh and for a moment he was able to appraise the source of his anxiety logically and asked himself which of the difficulties he faced could he do anything about? He leaned forward and rested his head in his hands as he realised that Rob and Charlie and Jenny were in God's hands, if there were one, and not his own.

At the far end of the garden was a narrow crazy-paved path. He stood up and walked towards it. Thorns and nettles lay either side. It was a mess and a pity because it led to the most perfect view of pastures well-tended by his neighbour. He breathed deeply. There was a way, he realised, of relieving himself of his anxiety concerning the canal. He confronted the solution with trepidation. He had tried to control the situation by lying. Why not give control to the police, where it belonged, and volunteer the truth? Once done, he would have to trust the police to recognise that it was the truth and that when he had struck the stranger on the canal he was acting in reasonable self-defence. Tell the police everything and let them get on with their job, then he could clear his mind and focus on the family. Would he tell them that Gracia was with him? A tough one. But, yes, he supposed he would, if he had to, yes.

There it was. How did he feel now? Better. The relief of knowing that he had found the way to unshoulder at least part of his burden was as refreshing as spring water. God, if he was still there, and a decent DI willing, the police may be annoyed but there was just a possibility that they might not prosecute him for having wasted their time.

Patrick turned and walked back to the house. Charlie's light was still on. The dogs sighed as he passed their beds on the way through to the sitting room.

He drained his glass and looked at the carriage clock on the mantelpiece. 4:30am, but it was an unreliable timepiece. He would ring Gray in the morning.

EASTER SUNDAY 21st APRIL 2019

MANCHESTER SQUARE, MARYLEBONE

8:15am

The party mood suggested by Gracia's selection of food for dinner had died by the time she came back downstairs. Gray had quietly laid the table, as she cooked in silence. "More wine?" he suggested.

"No, I'm OK thanks." She placed a large steaming pan of noodles and prawns on the table. Their discussion throughout the meal was amicable and trivial, based almost entirely on what they were eating. Gray had offered to wash up. Gracia had said she was tired and they both had an early night.

He slept badly, his mind unable to settle. Eventually, in the small hours, he fell into a deep sleep but he awoke at his usual early hour feeling so groggy and unrefreshed that he had stayed in bed. He turned on the radio but all he could find to tune into were celebrations of religious joy. Not in the mood, he turned it off again and dozed, only to be awoken by the buzzing of his phone on the bedside table. Only one person could be ringing at that time on Easter Sunday. Patrick did not wait for him to say hello.

"Gray, have I woken you up?"

"Patrick. Thank God. No, not at all. Glad to hear from you. How is Rob? How are you all?"

Without emotion, Patrick brought him fully up to date. Gray recognised the gravity of the situation.

"He is a young man, Patrick, he has that on his side."

"Yes, quite. We just have to hope for the best. I think that is what Jenny finds so difficult, not being able to do anything herself."

"It's good that you are all together, Patrick."

"Indeed."

"Patrick, this couldn't be more untimely, but we need to talk about that business on the canal. I am afraid there has been a development."

"Yes, I know."

Gray was surprised. "Oh, have you spoken to Gracia?"

"No. Have you?"

Gray took a breath.

"Well yes, I have actually. She stayed last night. I'm sorry, what have you heard?"

"I understand the police might have placed Gracia at the scene of the canal. It's just what I was trying to avoid. But she's spoken to you, has she?"

Gray could hear the strain in Patrick's voice. Hating the need to discuss a further difficulty for the poor man, he felt he had to bring him up to date.

"They called her in yesterday to show the CCTV footage from the night you were on the canal path together. You've seen it too, I gather?"

"Yes I have. Do you know how they've come to the conclusion that it is Gracia?"

Gray spoke carefully.

"I think so. A couple of days ago one of the tabloids published photos of her online. From what Gracia has said I believe the police have compared the CCTV and the tabloid images and concluded she is the woman who was with you. Gracia has denied it. Unfortunately, she also said that she was with me at the time, though of course she was not."

Patrick's sigh was deep and long. Gray wished to be able to tell him to forget the whole thing and concentrate on Rob. He couldn't.

"This body, Patrick. Gracia tells me that it's the person who attacked you. Do the police know yet about the dust up you had?"

Patrick was apologetic.

"I'm afraid not, Gray. I should have told them. Sorry, can you just hold on for a moment?"

Gray heard a muffled "Ten minutes?" Patrick returned.

"Sorry, Gray. Listen I'm obviously going to need to clear this up. Initially I just thought Gracia and I had had a bit of a to-do with a drunk and the police didn't need to know about it." He paused.

Gray made it easy for him. "Yes, quite. I understand that."

Patrick continued. "The trouble was, Gray, I didn't tell them everything. Not about Gracia being there, nor about the assault. It just seemed simpler. I wanted to keep her out of it, apart from anything else. But it's obviously different now. It's getting too complicated and I can't have this going on, not now, with everything here. I need to give the police all the facts. Is Gracia still with you?"

Gray confirmed that she was.

"Gray, I wonder if you might try to get her on board to tell the police what happened by the canal. So that we are both singing from the same hymn sheet, as it were?" He broke off and shouted. "I'm coming!" I'm sorry I am going to have to go. I'm sorry to put this on you, but would you mind? Coming! Sorry Gray, I have to go."

Gray returned his phone to the bedside table and pushed aside his duvet. He was aghast that Patrick, whose judgement and honesty he had trusted wholeheartedly for so many years, could be in such a mess.

Everything in Gray's mind told him that what Patrick suggested he do was right. The police should know the truth. But did Patrick realise the jeopardy he placed himself in by admitting now that he had lied? Gray sat down on the side of the bed and dropped his head. And Gracia.

An hour later she sat in the snug wearing his old dressing gown, her feet tucked beneath her, as usual. Her hands circled a mug of hot coffee. The expression on her face reminded him of how she had looked as a teenager constrained to defend herself against some complaint or other he had received from school.

"What have I done?"

He told her that Patrick had rung and that Rob's condition was still precarious. She looked down and pulled at a loose thread in the towelling.

"I'm so sorry."

He went to the point.

"The thing is, Gracia, this whole canal episode has become a bit of a mess. Patrick has a lot on his plate at the moment. He wants to set the record straight."

She shrugged.

"Well he can then, if he wants to. I told him he should tell the police about the assault at the start. But that doesn't have to involve me, does it?"

Gray looked at her. His eyes were honest and clear.

"If he is going to be completely truthful, as he wants to be, then yes it does. As I understand it you are the only witness to what happened when the man attacked him, do you see? Without you, if Patrick says he was involved in any kind of physical altercation with the man he rather lays himself open."

"Open to what?"

"Open to the possibility of the police determining that he was responsible for the man's death in some way, apart from anything else."

"But he wasn't."

Gray remained silent. He needed her to work out for herself how important it was that she assist.

Gracia's head lolled to one side in annoyance. She sighed.

"I went through all that with Patrick. If the police find out I was there it just puts me in the frame too. It doesn't help him."

She had made a good point. Gray took a breath to speak. She stopped him.

"Gray, you totally know how much shit I'm in already because of fucking Claudio. You know that this is absolutely the last thing I need at the moment. All I did that night was end a relationship and walk home. I feel really bad for Patrick cos of Rob, of course I do. It's awful for him. And if I thought I could help him in this way, then maybe I would, I don't know. But I genuinely don't think I can and I definitely don't want to throw myself under a bus with him, just for the sake of it."

Gray ran his fingers over the arm of his chair.

"Gracia, if the police came here and asked me if you were here with me that Thursday evening, what would you expect me to say?" He looked to her.

She got it.

"Oh, so you're saying you're not going to back me up? You're going to take Patrick's side and if they ask if I was here you're going to say no. Basically, you'll tell them I've lied." She stood up. "I might as well pack my toothbrush now, mightn't I? Or do they provide them for you in prison?"

Gray stood up to face her. He put his hands on her shoulders. She shrugged them off angrily and turned her back. He tried to reason.

"Gracia, you are right. You did do nothing wrong. You are an innocent witness and it would help everyone, not only Patrick but the police also, to know that. It is wrong to give a false alibi and in my position I simply can't lie to back you up. I can't. You must see that."

She revolted to face him, her eyes bright with anger.

"No Gray. It's not as simple as that. Patrick and I have been as bad as each other when it comes to what we've told the police. But surely things are better left as they are? Nothing happened and I wasn't there. Then neither of us has to go and admit we've lied. Whatever happened to land the bloke in the canal isn't anything to do with us anyway. If you back me up and agree that I was here and Patrick stays schtum, we're not involved. That's got to be better. He can focus on his family and I can get on with my life."

She moved towards the kitchen door then turned around and faced him. Her pretty blue eyes were stone cold hard with accusation.

"You know what, you're saying it'll help everyone if I tell the police. Well it won't actually, will it? I'll help the police maybe. And Patrick. And you. It helps everyone except me, actually, doesn't it? So, you know what, you've got a choice here. Are you willing to back me up? Or would you prefer to help Patrick clear his conscience, hang himself in the process and tell them I have lied? Which one of us matter to you most, Gray?"

JOHN RADCLIFFE HOSPITAL
1:00pm

Jenny knew there was no need for them to be at the hospital so soon. The operation was going to last at least a couple of hours. But where else would she want to be? Even though Rob was unconscious it was a comfort to be close by, a necessity in fact.

Charlie and Patrick weren't holding up too well. Charlie barely spoke other than to take orders for countless trips to the cafe, as if being helpful could somehow grant the atonement he denied himself. He showed every sign of having settled in his mind that he alone was responsible. Even the news that the motorcyclist had survived the accident had failed to cheer him. Charlie had done all he could to make himself feel worse, enquiring whether the rider had young children, was he self-employed, were his parents alive, would he be able to walk properly again, play sport, run and climb, even though no-one knew whether or not those were activities the man wanted to do. It was as if the worst case scenario was what Charlie had wanted to hear in order to justify his own self-loathing. When he had been told that the biker was a single man in his thirties with a safe job, few outdoor interests and that his prognosis was good, Charlie had settled into a deeper gloom as he was forced to make the effort to seek other avenues of blame.

As for Patrick, his reaction was less consistent. On Friday and Saturday morning he had reassured and comforted Jenny, repeated and attempted to clarify the parts of the surgeon's post-operative explanation that she had failed to remember or understand. But then his mood had changed. He became morose, almost snappy. He had taken a phone call and shouted at the caller that his son was critically ill in hospital and to leave him alone. Then he had calmed down, apologised and turned to her. "It's the police. They need a statement from Charlie." Later he told her that he had managed to persuade the accident investigators to come to the house to save Charlie having to go to the police station.

Today he was less agitated but seemed to be somehow distracted. They waited in their usual chairs in the relatives' room. Charlie had gone off on one of his needless errands to the cafe.

Patrick put his hand on her knee. "You know I love you, Jenny." This was a surprise. Gestures like that were no longer a regular feature of their marital vocabulary.

She placed her hand on top of his. "Of course I do."

He went on. "It's just that you need to know. We might have a lot to deal with and it may not be possible to say."

She had tried to smile reassuringly but failed and felt her face go all wrong.

"Shush love, you're tired."

"No really. Because ... oh, I don't know."

He stopped. Jenny had no idea what this was all about. Charlie came back with two cups of tea. She looked up at him and smiled.

"Thank you darling."

Charlie's eyes could not meet hers.

She turned to Patrick. "Here, tea. It'll make you feel better. Then why not shut your eyes for a bit. You've hardly slept."

The tea was lukewarm and watery. Patrick drank two mouthfuls then got up and said he was going outside to get some air.

MANCHESTER SQUARE, MARYLEBONE

2:00pm

Gracia had left an hour ago.

"You make me sick, you know that? See what I did? For one second I let myself think that you might finally be on my side. Joking wasn't I? When push comes to shove I'm on my own. Should be used to it, shouldn't I?"

She went upstairs and returned with a packed bag which she heaved onto her shoulder as she walked across the hall. The knocker clattered as she slammed the front door behind her. The giant chocolate egg he had bought for her lay unopened on the kitchen worktop.

He walked around the house, sat down in the snug, stood up, made a cup of coffee, didn't drink it, couldn't settle. Every object in the house was a distraction and he needed to think. He took his coat from the peg by the door and started walking.

In terms of public duty the issue was simple. Patrick should tell the police the truth and so should Gracia. They should give all the facts and then have faith in the police to conclude that the truth was that they were not responsible for the man's death.

But Gray knew that the truth is not tangible and is not always recognised for what it is. He knew that in the context of criminal trials, which are often litigated long after the events under scrutiny have passed, an account which is determined to be the ultimate truth is, in fact, no more than an accumulation of subjective and coincidental beliefs, formed by a jury whose members are selected at random.

Leaving aside cases in which witnesses deliberately lie, contradictory accounts of the same incident can be given by witnesses who fervently believe that they are telling the truth. In other words, their version of the truth is subjective also. Cross examination and other evidence are vital signposts to which version of the truth is the most reliable. That determination is made by juries. They have to consider the totality of the evidence and, from the morass of conflicting accounts which are sworn before them to be true, find a version that satisfies them beyond reasonable doubt. The process is complex and difficult. It becomes easier when a witness is shown to have lied, easier still when he or she admits that they have done so.

Gray was getting carried away. Patrick and Gracia were not on trial.

Nonetheless, should they follow the right course and change their statements, the police would take into account that they had both lied in their initial interviews. The average human being, never mind the average policeman, would be likely to treat any further statement by either of them with the utmost circumspection. The police would understandably assume that Patrick and Gracia had lied initially in order to cover up a truth that they were still concealing, which was that they were implicated in the man's death.

Which led Gray to wonder if he himself should believe that Patrick had been as innocent in the incident as he was saying. He banished the unworthy doubt from his mind. Gracia had described the attack the very next day, at a time when she was feeling far from well-disposed towards Patrick. That was reason enough to believe her when she said that Patrick had simply defended himself, and her too, against an attacker. Once again, Gray dismissed the thought that Patrick had lied to him, guiltily admonishing himself for questioning Patrick's story. If he couldn't believe Patrick, who would he ever believe about anything? Had almost a decade on the Bench rendered him so sceptical as to doubt even the most reliable truth teller? His mind was wandering. He needed to consider the facts.

By coming forward with a new story, Patrick, and Gracia too if she were to support him, would be laying themselves open to arrest, intense scrutiny, the risk of charges of wasting police time or, far worse, perverting the course of justice, manslaughter, murder even. There was no guarantee whatsoever that they would walk free. Did Patrick realise all this?

So was Gracia right? Would they both be better advised to stick to their original account, untrue though it was, in order to save the trouble of trying to prove their innocence because, make no bones about it, realistically that is what they would have to do once they admitted their earlier engagement with the dead man.

Gracia. Poor Gracia. She had had to deal with loss and grief as a child and elbowed her way to the brink of success despite a weight of personal baggage. And now, at last, it had looked as if she might be about to be happy. If she were to be believed, and why not, she was entirely innocent in the matter of the canal death. She'd given a false alibi. Did she deserve to lose everything for that?

And Patrick? Even as Gray walked the streets, past shops, houses and office buildings which made no impact on his consciousness, Patrick was staring the death of his son in the face? Could he take any more?

What of Gray's own responsibility? Surely, irrespective of the personal consequences that might entail, he was right to encourage them both to take the course suggested by Patrick and come clean. He had spent his whole professional life as a judge having to close down his emotional response to the parties' circumstances.

He recalled a case in which a man, blinded by childhood meningitis, had attended a garden party at a house in Richmond on Thames. The host was an arrogant, loud-mouthed City banker who had warned both the blind man and his wife that there was no fence between the bottom of the garden and the river. Late in the evening the partygoers had moved indoors. Most people had been drinking all afternoon. The blind man took a stroll in the garden. He was unaccompanied and, having lost his bearings, fell into the river. He did not die. It would have been better if he had done since lack of oxygen during the time he spent in the water caused substantial brain damage. Gray's heart had gone out to the man and his devoted, guilt-ridden wife, but Gray had had to find that the blind man's decision to walk alone in an unfamiliar space without heeding his host's initial warning rendered him contributorily negligent and thus not entitled to the full sum of compensation he claimed. The City banker had triumphantly punched the air when Gray gave his judgment. The blind man's wife had led her husband quietly away.

But now Gray found himself having to make a decision which would affect the two people he loved most in the world rather than litigants about whom he could be dispassionate. It felt very different.

Never mind that, what about loyalty? The problem was that there was no compromise. In order to support Patrick he would, if necessary, tell the police that Gracia had not been with him on the night in question. To support Gracia he would do the opposite. If the police contacted him, and surely they would, he had to decide one way or the other. If he took Patrick's course he would lose Gracia's trust forever and break his moral commitment to stand by her when all others fell away. How supportive was he, now, when she needed him? On the other hand, could he let Patrick down? The words "I will do anything I can to help" were devoid of meaning if they did not include telling the truth when asked to do so.

And never mind all this. Returning to the central question – should he tell the truth or not – it was one thing to know in theory what he should do. It would be quite another to do it. If he asked himself the same question as he had asked Gracia "What shall I say if the police ask if you were with me during the evening of April 4th?" he knew that he would need to answer "No. I am afraid she has got that wrong." But it was impossible to imagine himself doing that. It was equally impossible to imagine himself lying.

Subconsciously, he had reached the Temple. The buildings were dark. The courtyards and lanes silently waiting for the purposeful to-ing and fro- ing of barristers, clerks and lawyers who populated them during the week. He loved this space. He walked up to Middle Temple garden and looked over at the neat lawns and tidy flower beds. A robin was chirruping in a tree nearby. Its cheerful song gladdened Gray's heart for a second or two.

"Gray?" A woman's voice from behind. Familiar.

He turned to see Vanessa, inclining slightly towards him, a question in her eyes.

"It is you. Hello! Happy Easter!" She was dressed casually in trousers and jacket. Her hair was shorter, face possibly a little fuller, but the kindly expression was unchanged. She was accompanied by two boys.

Involuntarily, his spirits lifted.

"Vanessa! Good heavens, hello! What are you doing here?"

"I thought it was time the boys saw the Temple. They are singularly unimpressed. Nick, Chris, say hello. This is Gray."

The boys obeyed. They looked to be young teenagers. One was taller, dark haired. The younger one had Vanessa's softness of feature and pepper and salt hair colour.

Vanessa. The woman who had understood that insecurity was Gracia's problem and total possession of Gray her only cure. Vanessa, who so long ago, had loved him. He yearned for the boys to disappear, for her to sit next to him and give him wise counsel. Instead he was forced to make small talk. She was still working: family law – children – adoption, wardship, care proceedings. The boys were twelve and ten, growing fast, eating her out of house and home. They were looking forward to senior school. She'd brought them out for some air after a big lunch.

She did not mention her husband.

But how about Gray? How was Gracia? He told her about *Initiate*.

"Yes, I've heard of it. Haven't seen it yet. The children aren't old enough, are you?" The older boy had rolled his eyes. He was definitely old enough.

After ten minutes the boys were showing signs of boredom, pinching each other and playing an apparently pointless but distracting and attention-seeking game which involved pushing and tripping each other up. Gray sensed that Middle Temple garden had failed their mother's promise of interest and he, the old man on the bench, was the icing on the cake of ennui. Fondly, he and she exchanged goodbyes.

As she walked away, Gray heard one of the boys ask "Who was that?"

"He's a High Court judge. Probably one of the cleverest people you'll ever meet." Vanessa had replied. "And nicest." But Gray did not hear that bit.

He turned around and began to walk back home, a little cheered but no further toward finding the way to enlighten his muddled mind.

WEST HADDON

11:50pm

Patrick said goodnight to Jenny and went back downstairs. For a few minutes he just wanted to sit, that was all. The dogs strolled into the sitting room and flopped down sleepily on the floor next to him. Patrick roughed the scruff of Billy's neck with his feet, shut his eyes and lost himself to the peace and quiet.

Rob had been taken down into theatre just after 4:00pm. Some hours later Mr Al-Shaater had come in to see them. His face was inscrutable.

"Mr and Mrs Kingdom, I'm sorry you've had to wait."

They waved the apology aside. Of course they understood.

"Shall we all sit down?"

Patrick sensed that this was a prelude to bad news. He sat beside Jenny and took her hand. Charlie remained standing at a distance.

During his account of Rob's operation, the outcome and future prognosis, the surgeon periodically closed his eyes in concentration, nodding occasionally as if in affirmation of his own accuracy.

He told them that, on examination, once the dressings had been removed from Rob's abdomen, the lesions in the liver were obviously not yet healed but there had been no further bleeding. That was the outcome he had hoped for. Rob's incisions had been stitched and he was now back in the ICU where, in due course, he would regain consciousness.

The surgeon paused and looked at them. No one spoke for a second.

Jenny was the first to react.

"So, he's going to be OK?"

The surgeon replied carefully.

"We have to take things very slowly. For now we have to wait a while to ensure that Rob's condition is stable. I am sorry, all this waiting is very difficult for you. We will know more in a few hours. For now I just wanted to tell you that the operation had gone well and that our findings have all been positive."

He went on to say that Rob's underlying good health and youth were both factors in his favour but that they must be aware that Rob's condition was still serious.

Patrick now understood why they had been asked to sit down. Jenny fell forward, her elbows on her knees, hands covering her face as her shoulders heaved uncontrollably. When she looked up she looked elated but exhausted. She apologised. Then she had a thousand questions. Patrick could tell that the surgeon just wanted them to take one step at a time. But Rob wasn't his child.

Mr Al-Shaater told them that someone would let them know as soon as Rob came round. Jenny stood up. For a ghastly moment Patrick thought she was going to hug the man who had so far saved her son's life. She didn't, but she thanked him over and over again. Patrick felt it was too soon. Had she understood that Rob was still in a serious condition? He wondered if the same thought was in the surgeon's mind. Mr Al-Shaater backed towards the door, gave a half smile and left them alone.

"More tea? Or shall we celebrate with hot chocolate?" said Charlie.

By the time Rob's nurse came into the room, time had dragged its way to the middle of the evening. She told them that Rob was awake. He was still very drowsy but they could go and see him for a short while. She said she was really sorry but only two of them were allowed in at once.

Charlie looked at his parents. "You two go."

Patrick looked back at his stricken son. "No Charlie, you go with Mum. He'll be glad to see that you're OK."

They didn't stay long. When they came back Jenny was smiling. "Go in, just for a bit, Patrick. He's very woozy, but he'll know who you are."

Patrick went in. Rob looked no different, still surrounded by tubes, machines and functional bedding. Patrick gently put his hand onto his son's wrist. Rob's eyes opened. "Dad." he said. That was all.

They got home late. One of Jenny's church friends had left a note. "Dogs fed and walked. Praying for you."

EASTER MONDAY 22nd APRIL 2019

WEST HADDON

7:30am

At some time in the middle of the night Patrick had gone up to bed. Birdsong now filtered into the room from the garden. He opened his eyes and looked at Jenny. She was lying on her side with her back to him. Beneath her linen pyjama top, her shoulders looked tense, even in repose. Hardly surprising. Patrick rolled onto his back, reached for his phone and sent a text:

Gray. Rob still in ICU but improving. We have hope. P.

He tried to get out of bed without waking Jenny but she turned over and opened her eyes.

"What's the time?" she asked.

"Half seven."

She sat up instantly. "Has the hospital rung?"

"No. We'll get up and go straight there, do you think?"

"Of course." She threw the duvet aside and put her feet on the floor.

"Jenny, if Rob's OK today I ought to go down to London tomorrow. Not for long though. I'll pick up some work and bring it back."

"OK" she said, on her way to the en suite for a shower. A text came back from Gray.

Good news indeed. Thank you for keeping me up to date. G

ANGEL

11:00am

"It's the Bank Holiday! What are you doing?"

Caz Sanders had to shout above the vacuum cleaner. She was standing at the door to her sister's bedroom. She couldn't see Jayne but the regular appearance and disappearance of the brush extension from beneath the bed indicated that she was somewhere on the other side of it. A bottle of Windolene stood on the window sill with a cloth beside it. The entire surface of Jayne's crowded dressing table had been cleared. Bottles, pots, brushes and hair bobbles, makeup, lanyard and photographs were piled onto her bed, which had been stripped of linen.

Jayne stood up, flushed and sweating. Strands of hair had escaped from the scrunchie which held her ponytail. She swept the back of her wrist over her sticky forehead and switched off the vacuum. "What?"

Her sister looked at her, an enormous question mark in her eyes. "What's going on?"

Jayne laughed.

"This, little sister, is called cleaning your room. Try it one day."

Caz laughed back.

"No way! Why?!"

Jayne placed the end of the brush extension carefully to the left side of her feet, then kicked it into the air. It described a perfect arc and fell into her right hand. It would have been a moment of pure cabaret if her attire had been top hat and tails as opposed to sweatpants, sloppy top and rubber gloves.

"Because I am very angry and extremely frustrated with my dimwit partner, Mr Jalal Malek, see?"

She restarted the vacuum and set about the curtains. Caz held up her hands in horror.

"No stop! This is way too much stress. Why? I thought you liked him?"

Jayne turned the vacuum back off and looked at her. She blew air through her lips, making them reverberate noisily.

"I do. But he is such a twat."

Caz usually told her to shut up whenever Jayne moaned about work but, for once, she told her sister to go on.

"It's so obvious. The body in the canal case, right? We're under huge pressure to get it resolved quickly, right? Patrick Kingdom, he's this big lawyer right, is lying. We've got a witness. Him and Gracia Peel – yeah, Gracia Peel – are together on the canal, and they've both lied about it and said she's not there at all. I mean, come on? Why would they lie? Oh wait." She pointed her right forefinger into the air and wagged her head. "Maybe it's because there's a dead body floating in the canal, just where they've been. Maybe that is something to do with it."

Caz was glad she hadn't told her sister to shut up.

"Gracia Peel! Wait, you interviewed Gracia Peel? Why didn't you say?"

"I am saying?"

"Well, what was she like?"

"Bitch actually."

"Seriously?"

"Yeah." Jayne shut her sister down, not in the mood for celebrity gossip. "Okay? So what's Jal done wrong?"

Jayne picked up a cloth and began wiping her dressing table. "He's done nothing. That's what. Nothing."

She turned around, leant against the table and held her right elbow in her left hand as she pointed at, underlined and illustrated every aspect of her frustration with her forefinger.

"On Saturday, right, this other witness basically says, 'Yeah that's Gracia Peel,' but Jal, instead of saying, 'Right, we'll bust them', looks at his watch and says, 'No Jayne, we're going to wait till after the holiday.' I mean come ON? By Tuesday Mr Swankypants QC Patrick Kingdom will have his story well sorted out, and so will Miss Famous Actress Gracia Peel. It's fiction. He's a barrister, she's an actress. Their whole lives are make-believe. We should have gone straight round and caught at least one of them off their guard. That was our best chance. But no. Jalal decides it's Easter Bunny time because Jalal Malek is a lazy sod and couldn't be arsed. So, what I am doing now is reasserting some control over my life and cleaning my bedroom, get it?"

Point made, she glared at her sister.

Caz held her hands up, palms forward. "Chill OUT sister. You're mental, you do know that, right?" And left the room as the vacuum buzzed back into action.

TUESDAY 23rd APRIL

WEST HADDON

8:30am

Dressed in dark suit and leather shoes, Patrick walked through the kitchen and picked up his car keys. Jenny stood at the island chopping celery for a salad to take to the hospital.

Normally, Patrick was blessed with the gift of being able to sleep well, regardless of anxiety or the pressures of the day ahead. Only movement disturbed him and Jenny's repeated turns from front to back to side then other side in her unfulfilled quest for a restful position told him that she had spent many sleepless hours since Friday. Last night it had seemed that she had slept soundly for the first time. There was good reason. Rob's condition had remained stable. Mr Al-Shaater had done his best to restrain their optimism. He had told them that they must not get ahead of themselves but the fact that Rob was now conscious and breathing on his own was remarkable progress. There was a long way to go. Nevertheless, with patience and time, rigorous physiotherapy and careful management, a full recovery was now possible.

Jenny looked up as her husband passed through to the back door.

"When will you be back?"

Patrick calculated. He needed to go to Chambers, the flat and then the police station, depending on when Malek and Sanders could see him. He was reluctant to tie himself down.

"I'm not sure. Depends on the traffic. I'll go straight to the hospital."

Billy and Bunter raised their eyebrows at him as he passed their beds. He called back.

"Is someone coming to walk the dogs?"

"Yes, don't worry. See you later."

He turned the car on the gravel and drove out onto the country lane. It was another sunny day but could just as well have been snowing for all the notice he took of the weather.

THE ROYAL COURTS OF JUSTICE

8:30am

The RCJ building was quieter than usual. The majority of courts do not sit during the week after Easter but one court is always open for emergency applications and Gray was the judge designated to be present and ready to preside for the rest of the week. He was glad to be away from home where the atmosphere was charged with pressure. Ruefully he acknowledged to himself the irony of finding respite in his work, the nature of which required him to make difficult decisions almost daily.

"Good holiday, sir?" Neil greeted him. "Coffee?"

"Thank you, Neil." Gray sat at his desk and opened his laptop. There was comfort in seeing emails that didn't matter. Then he turned his mind to the judgment he had to write. It was an appeal from the county court.

Maddie Collins, aged twenty-two, had been walking around the perimeter path of her local park when she was struck in the face by a cricket ball which had been hit for a magnificent six by a batsman on the square in the centre of the park. Maddie had suffered a fractured cheekbone and unsightly alteration to the composition of her face. She had sued the local council. Gray had had to decide whether the council's duty of care to users of the park extended to erecting a fence or putting signage along the path to warn them of flying cricket balls or, alternatively, whether it was up to Maddie and other walkers to keep their wits about them. The county court judge had decided in Maddie's favour and the council had appealed. Gray had decided to uphold the original decision that the council were liable for Maddie's injuries. His task today was to set his conclusion down in writing, supported by earlier rulings of the Court of Appeal.

Neil came in half an hour later and stood just inside the door.

"I'm sorry to interrupt sir, but there has been a request from Islington Police Station for a couple of officers to come in to see you some time today, if it is convenient, concerning an incident that occurred on the Regent's Canal earlier this month?"

Gray had been so absorbed in the monetary valuation of Maddie Collins's injuries and disfigurement that he took a second to register the enormity of what Neil was asking.

"Today?" he asked.

"I got that impression, sir, yes."

Gray looked at his laptop, then back to Neil. Get it over with.

"See if they can be here in an hour."

Neil had acquiesced and retired discreetly from the room. He was adept at recognising when Gray wanted him to ask no more questions.

WEST HADDON

9:00am

Jenny was upstairs when the doorbell rang. She had forgotten that Anthea, the dog walker, was coming and ran down. To save unbolting the front door she shouted:

"I'll bring them out the back. Hold on."

From the utility room she gathered the necessary accessories. The dogs sprang from their beds in joyful recognition of routine preparations for a walk. Jenny opened the back door and looked around for Anthea. Billy and Bunter pushed past her legs and bounded round to the front of the house, barking territorially. Rounding the corner after them she saw a police car parked on the gravel. Two young constables, both in uniform, were standing a short distance from the stone steps leading to the front door. One was carrying a large black electrical appliance. Bunter held an irrational and strong aversion to men who came to the house dressed in black trousers, meaning almost all men, particularly those carrying objects he did not recognise. He was snapping aggressively round the intruders' legs in heightened rage at the invasion of his domain, backed up stolidly by his brother, Billy. The constables appeared to be terrified.

"Bunter! Billy! Stop it!"

Jenny ran to the dogs and grabbed their collars to restrain their stocky onslaught.

"I'm so sorry. It's your trousers," she explained.

The constable nearest to Bunter's slavering mouth looked in bemusement at his legs, as she continued. "I'll put them inside. Dogs, come on!"

She made an ungainly return to the house and hustled both dogs indoors. The constables remained hesitantly beside their car until she returned.

"I'm so sorry about that. Um. How can I help?"

One of the constables told her that they were accident investigators and reminded her that they had spoken to Patrick on Saturday and made an appointment to come at this time today to take a statement from Charles Kingdom regarding the road traffic accident he had been involved in on Friday.

Jenny's hand went to the top of her head, her fingers clenching her hair. "Oh heavens. I am so sorry. We had completely forgotten. You'd better come in."

They followed her into the kitchen where she tried to gather her wits. Charlie was still in bed. Should she wake him and let him talk to the police on his own? He had been so determined to blame himself, it did not feel safe to do that. She looked to the two young men. They appeared to be about the same age as Rob, maybe a bit older. Their expressions suggested openness and a hint of pity for her discomposure.

"Look, I'm so sorry. We are all over the place here. Charlie is not really up yet. Our other son is in hospital, in intensive care. I was just on my way. I need to talk to my husband. He's on his way to London. Can you hold on? I might just get him before he catches the train."

Without waiting for their answer, she walked out of the kitchen dialling Patrick's number, leaving the constables looking warily at the dogs who, defeated in the battle of their patch, were back in bed, sulking.

Patrick answered from the station platform.

"Christ, Jenny, I'll have to come back. Give them a cup of tea and get Charlie up. Will you be able to go to the hospital on your own? Don't let them start till I get back though. I'll be half an hour."

ISLINGTON POLICE STATION

9:00am

Jayne had got in to work early. She put her bag down onto her desk and looked around. Jalal's chair was empty. Good. He could not impede the progress she intended to make in checking out Gracia Peel's alibi. Having repeatedly compared the tabloid images with the CCTV footage, Jayne was certain that Peel was the woman with Patrick Kingdom on the crossing to Primrose Hill. James Mitchell's recollection of hearing Peel's characteristic "Neeugh" expletive on the canal path bolstered her certainty. Peel had said she was with the High Court judge so the obvious next step was to interview him. Should she check with the DS first before contacting him? Normally she would, no doubt about it. But Cartwright's 'nannying' criticism still stung so she had left it. She had got through to the judge's clerk on the phone and arranged to meet the judge at the Royal Courts of Justice at 9.30 am. The clerk gave her directions to the side entrance and told her that she would be met there.

Jalal arrived at his desk punctually, shortly before 9:00am. Triumphantly, Jayne announced her progress. Jalal did not have time to protest before his phone rang. "DC Malek here. Good morning, sir. I see. Yes, that would be fine. What time would you like to come in? Four o'clock? We will see you then. Goodbye."

He replaced the phone, looked at Jayne and spoke, somewhat churlishly.

"Patrick Kingdom wants to see us. He's coming in at four."

She looked back, incredulously. "Did you ask why?" Jalal said no, he did not. "Come on then, we'd better not be late for the judge. I'll drive."

The dogs sprang delightedly from their beds. Patrick's arrival at the back door finally meant that it was time for their walk. They muddled and snorted happily around his legs as he regarded the scene in the kitchen. It was almost charming. Two pastel-coloured mugs, a matching milk jug and plate of biscuits were placed on the kitchen table. Jenny was leaning with her back against the Aga, holding her own mug in both hands. The gentility of the portrait was spoiled, however, by the two constables seated stiffly on the pine, spindle-backed chairs with a large portable recording device on the table before them. They half rose to their feet as Patrick entered.

"Don't get up," he said briskly.

They sat back down again and Jenny introduced them. "Darling. This is PC Tebbutt and PC Edwards."

Patrick looked towards them. "Yes, hello." Then he turned to Jenny. "Where's Charlie?"

"He'll be down in a minute." Patrick turned to their visitors.

"I am so sorry to have kept you waiting. You've probably gathered we've had a lot on our minds this weekend. I'm afraid I had completely forgotten that you were coming. But obviously this is important. You are here to take a statement from Charlie about the accident, is that right?"

"Yes, sir." PC Tebbutt or PC Edwards, neither Jenny nor Patrick knew which was which, nodded.

After a minute or two of stilted conversation about traffic and how easy it had been for the constables to find the house, the door from the hall opened. Charlie walked slowly in, a tousle-haired picture of apprehension, barefoot in track suit bottoms and T-shirt. His left arm was supported by a sling. He eyed the constables nervously, "Um hello. I'm Charlie." The constables half stood up and then sat down again.

The three young men were of similar age. In different circumstances they might be having a pint and a laugh together in the village pub. This situation could not have been less convivial.

Patrick took command. "Charlie, why don't you get yourself something to eat?"

Charlie looked to the constables. One of them gave an amiable nod as Jenny suggested Charlie have some coffee too and fussed around in the cupboard for a mug and cereal bowl.

Patrick addressed the policemen once more.

"I need to have a quick word with Charlie in private first, if you don't mind.

And I'll sit in. My wife may have told you I'm a lawyer?"

"Yes sir." The constables stood up, indicating a willingness to wait outside.

Billy and Bunter sprang up, poised for exercise.

Charlie looked up from pouring his cereal.

"You could take the dogs out in the garden if you like. There are some tennis balls by the back door. If you throw them, they love chasing them."

Jenny suggested the constables stay where they were and that Patrick and Charlie go somewhere else private.

Patrick guided his son into the sitting room where they sat together on one of the sofas.

"Now listen to me, Charlie. This is what's going to happen. It looks like they are going to record the interview. They'll talk you through how that works I'm sure but we all introduce ourselves and then you will be cautioned. Do you know what that means?"

Charlie did. He'd watched enough TV dramas. "OK. Then they will ask you what happened." Charlie looked down. Patrick spoke kindly.

"Charlie, listen. I know you blame yourself but all I am asking is that you don't exaggerate what you think you did wrong. It won't help Rob and it certainly won't help you. The most important thing is that you be as truthful as you can. If you don't know something then just say so, or take a moment and don't speak until you're happy with what you are going to tell them. I'll be with you and if I feel they're pushing you too hard or ask anything unreasonable, I'll stop them, OK?"

Charlie nodded and sighed, rubbing his finger and thumb around the piping of the upholstered cushion beside him. "Will I go to prison, Dad? I mean, I know I deserve it, but Mum? And you? I'm just so sorry."

Patrick put his hand on his son's knee and patted it in reassurance. "We are going to do everything we can to make sure that doesn't happen, OK? Take my advice, think before you speak and tell the truth. You can do this." He stood up. "Come on, chap."

In the kitchen the kettle was boiling again, and Jenny was spooning fresh grounds into the cafetière. She looked round.

"Patrick, I'm going to go to the hospital, OK? Ring me when you finish. OK Charlie?"

"Sure." Charlie replied.

Jenny made the coffee, smiled at Tebbutt and Edwards and picked up her car keys from the island.

The dogs stood up and walked to the door, tails wagging. Jenny spoke over her shoulder.

"I'll put them outside. Anthea should be here in a minute."

Gray waited. Neil was on his way up to his room with the police.

"In here."

Too soon, Neil's voice heralded the arrival of two policemen. One female, neat and athletic in appearance, the other male, older, shorter, fatter. Neither of them was in uniform, detectives. Gray stood up.

"Thank you Neil. Good afternoon officers, come and sit down." He indicated two chairs on the other side of his desk. "Would you like a cup of tea?"

He hoped they would decline. The length of time that it would take Neil to prepare tea would necessarily dictate a period of small talk for which he was far from being in the mood. The male detective replied with a polite "no thank you" on behalf of both of them and gave their names and ranks. Junior officers. Interesting. They sat upright on their chairs. The female removed a pocket book, pencil and a recording device from an inside pocket. Malek, the male, wasted no time in preliminaries.

"Thank you for seeing us, your um Honour."

My Lord, Sir, Judge. Any of those would have done as a form of address. Your Honour designates a Crown Court judge, one step of the ladder beneath Gray in the judicial hierarchy. It is not used outside the courtroom. Gray did not correct him.

DC Malek explained what Gray already knew. They were investigating a death which had occurred in the Regent's Canal on April 4th or 5th and were following up leads regarding persons who might have been on the canal path between St John's Wood and Primrose Hill on April 4th. He paused.

"Yes," said Gray.

"Can you tell us what you did on April 4th, Your Honour?"

Malek's repeated salutary gaff, combined with the unnecessarily long period to be accounted for - the whole of April 4th - gave Gray a momentary sense of advantage but he realised it would be short-lived. Sooner or later he would be required to answer, "Did Gracia Peel spend the evening with you?" however long it might take Malek to get round to it. Nevertheless he was thankful for the time he had been allowed.

"Off hand, I don't remember what exactly I did that day. Let me look. He tapped his tongue against his soft palate as he referred to the diary on his computer. "A Thursday, right?"

Malek nodded.

"Well I was here during the day. My diary doesn't say any more."

"So, would you have gone home after work?"

"Yes."

"Where is that, if you don't mind me asking?"

"Manchester Square, Marylebone."

Jalal acknowledged the impressiveness of Gray's address. "Nice."

"Very. Thank you," Gray responded.

"And that would have been at what time?"

"I don't keep a regular pattern. Around six perhaps. Five thirty? I work at home in the evenings, if I need to."

Malek's demeanour softened a little.

"I imagine that must happen quite often, Your Honour. This -" his hand wafted around the grandeur of Gray's surroundings, in an attempt to indicate the weight of work borne by its occupant "all this, can't just be nine to five?"

"Indeed."

Malek resumed.

"So, you left here sometime around five thirty, six possibly, and then?"

"I went home."

"Would that have been by car or taxi?"

Clearly the policeman did not envisage him taking the tube. Gray gave what he knew was irrelevant detail. Anything to delay the inevitable question.

"It will have depended on the weather. I'm afraid I can't remember what it was like that day. But if it was not raining I most likely walked."

"And which way would that have taken you, Your um?"

"Well not along the Regent's Canal. I have a choice of route but I never go that far north. Usually I go through Fitzrovia."

This clearly made sense and the male detective nodded. His counterpart sat back.

"So you would have got home at ..?"

Gray felt the timeline was becoming fictitious. He genuinely could not remember what time he had left court that day, or how he had travelled home, nor when he had arrived. Understanding that Malek was simply being as thorough as necessary, he explained this, as politely as possible.

Malek got it. "My apologies, Your Honour. However you travelled home that evening, and allowing for some leeway, would it be safe to say that you would most likely have been there by, say, half past six?"

Gray agreed that that would be safe but not certain.

Malek reached the point. "And do you remember how you spent that evening?"

This was it.

Gray swallowed. He looked, not at Malek, but at the female whose attention appeared to be drawn to the bookshelf behind Gray which, he recalled, bore a framed photograph of Gracia. Her pen hovered above the page of her notebook.

A tap. An unmistakeable tap at the door followed by another. Neil entered, not alone.

"Yes?" Gray inquired, with love in his heart.

Neil was accompanied by Richard Jevons, Queen's Bench Listing Officer, who, bearing a thick file of documents, spoke.

"I'm sorry to interrupt, sir, but there's an emergency application for an injunction. Counsel are in court. The Daily Mail intend to -"

Gray interrupted. "Sorry. Hold on a minute, Richard. Detective Constable Malek I'm sorry, would you mind stepping outside for a minute or two? Neil?" He looked to his clerk to remove the two policemen from the room.

"Richard, sorry, go on."

Malek, his partner and Neil once removed, Richard explained that the Daily Mail intended to print a story which revealed that a senior politician, now a member the House of Lords, had had links with a Soviet spy network during the Cold War. The politician was seeking an injunction to prevent publication. Indicating the weighty file he embraced, he intimated that there was a lot to read and that counsel were, of course, willing to wait until His Lordship was ready.

"Of course, Richard. Thank you." Gray appraised the file. "Give me an hour? Could you ask Neil to step back in."

Neil returned. "Sir?"

"Neil, please apologise to Detective Constable Malek and his partner, I'm sorry, I can't remember her name. I'm going to have to deal with this straight away. Tell them I'm going to be tied up for the rest of the morning at least and ask if I can ring later to reschedule our interview. Get the number, if you would."

Neil inclined his head and retired from the room as, with overwhelming relief at the respite gained, Gray addressed the far safer ground of freedom of the press.

ISLINGTON POLICE STATION

10:45am

They had not spoken during the drive. Back at her desk Jayne threw her bag onto her desk in frustration.

"We had him. We bloody had him."

Twenty minutes later they were summoned to Cartwright's office to give an update on the canal death. Jalal began. He explained that their investigations were currently focused on the movements of Patrick Kingdom as they had some concerns about the truth of his first statement, in particular regarding the identity of the woman with him on the canal, who they believed to be the actress, Gracia Peel. He summarised the information they had been given by James Mitchell and the CCTV evidence, and reported that they had interviewed Peel but she had denied being near the canal on April 4th. Jayne added that the abortive meeting with Sir Graham Andrew to verify Peel's alibi would be rescheduled as soon as possible.

It was apparent that Cartwright had eaten an energy bar some time shortly before their meeting. A piece of hazelnut dangled at the end of a strand of saliva from the centre of his lower lip. Several other pieces, together with microscopic chips of chocolate, were lodged in the corner of his mouth. The effect was nauseating. He raised his eyes, pinprick cold, to look from one constable to the other. Then he spoke.

"Have you lost your senses?"

Cartwright reached for his notes and sat back. The motion caused the saliva strand to sway hypnotically but it remained firmly in place. He summarised the constables' findings.

"If I am correct, the body of David McBrain is pulled from the canal on the morning of April 5th. He has sustained some injuries but the cause of death is drowning. It is hard to be precise about the time of death but it occurred sometime between approximately four pm on Thursday 4th April and six am the following morning when the body was seen in the canal by a passing cyclist. DNA matches prove that items of bedding and clothing belonging to McBrain had been left beneath Bridge No. 9. The blood alcohol level in his body is high. He had also taken spice."

Little spheres of spit accumulated on his bottom lip with the delivery of every sibilant. In reaction to the mess created by the word 'spice' he paused to wipe his mouth. He did so carelessly with the side of one forefinger and inadvertently avoided the fragment of hazelnut which trapezed from side to side.

"No eye witnesses have come forward nor has there been any result from the media appeal. The only witness to come forward at all is Mr James Mitchell, a barrister, who was running along the canal at approximately six forty-five pm on April 4th. Also known to have been on the canal path at that time were Mitchell's work colleague, Mr Patrick Kingdom QC, and a woman.

You have interviewed Mr Kingdom. He confirms he met Mr Mitchell and says the woman was a stranger who had asked for directions."

At this point the DS stopped reading, sat up and looked directly at Sanders and Malek, saliva shining on his chin.

"These facts have prompted the two of you to question a well-known actress in the hope of extracting an admission from her that she was the stranger who met Mr Kingdom on the canal. I will reiterate, the theory you are currently pursuing is that Mr Kingdom and Ms Gracia Peel were, in fact, acquaintances and not strangers. Though, where that would get you, even if true, I have yet to fathom. Not content with having interviewed Mr Kingdom – how many times, three is it? – not to mention Miss Peel herself, it is now your intention to re-interview a High Court judge, no less, to check that the actress and indeed Mr Kingdom are telling the truth. Your basis for believing that the woman on the canal is Miss Peel is little more than a similar haircut, items of clothing and a noise she apparently made. A noise? What do you propose next? A noise parade? Line her up with a few people and ask them to step in a puddle just so we can hear what noise they make? Can I ask you, DC Sanders, DC Malek, what planet you are on? Am I the only one in this room who thinks it is advisable NOT to harass senior members of the judiciary, the Bar, and celebrated actresses, all of whom have a direct line to the tabloids with all the bad press that they can shovel at the Metropolitan Police, unless absolutely necessary?"

Cartwright's desk was spattered with droplets of gob. He ran his shirt sleeved forearm over them as he waited for a reply. The piece of hazelnut now adhered to his tie.

A sense of injustice ballooned in Jayne's throat. He had TOLD them to get on and interview who they liked, the bastard. She said nothing. Malek also was silent.

"Am I?"

They spoke as one. "No, sir."

He stood up. "I am ordering the two of you to cease this line of enquiry here and now." And then continued. "Have you carried out a single interview with anyone who knew Mr McBrain, or who sleeps on the canal, or who sits there, unnoticed by ninety-nine per cent of the population and observes what happens there when no-one else is looking?"

Suicidally, in Jayne's opinion, Jalal intervened to remind the detective sergeant that he had spent a few hours on the canal on Friday afternoon but had made no significant progress.

Cartwright's response was withering. "How about you try a bit harder, DC

Malek? I am telling you both now to return to the canal. Go back and talk to the people there and, unless and until you have my express permission to do otherwise, leave everyone else – QCs, High Court judges, the cast of Lion King, the Pope – alone. Do you understand?"

"Sir" they said in embarrassed unison. Cartwright's tongue did a fat, flabby sweep of his lip. He wiped his chin with the back of his wrist and dismissed them.

Jayne was too livid to share with Jalal how grossed out she felt. Livid that Cartwright had made no acknowledgement of the clear 'get on with it and leave me alone.' message that he had delivered at the start of the enquiry, livid that she was being pulled up just as she was getting somewhere, livid with Jalal for having held her back. She'd be way further ahead by now if it had not been for him dragging his feet. She grabbed her coat and snapped, "Coming then?" He followed her, asking,

"What about Kingdom?"

She did not answer till they were in the car. "Kingdom wants to see us, doesn't he? Don't see why we have to do anything about that."

REGENT'S CANAL BETWEEN BRIDGE NO. 9 AND PRIMROSE HILL BRIDGE

MID MORNING

James had never been able to work out what made it easier to run on some days than others. This morning he felt strong and swift. The sun was warm, the ground dry and the path clear and uncluttered by the many cyclists who habitually disrupted his normal run to work.

He had set aside the day to prepare for a heavy trial which he was due to start on Wednesday at Southwark Crown Court but, having already done much of the work, was treating himself to a run round Regent's Park and back before getting down to it. He had established a good pace by the time he passed beneath Bridge No. 9. On each bank lay one or two silent mounds of grime-coloured sleeping bags and a single tent.

Shortly after that, he reached the graffitied section of wall and remembered the email he had sent to Patrick Kingdom. He looked forward to a jokey reply later. Although, maybe Patrick had never heard of Gracia Peel? Or maybe he knew exactly who she was? That would be interesting. James made a mental note to keep an eye out for Patrick later.

The police cordon had been removed and it was now possible to run straight along the canalside path without deviating to the upper route, but the witness appeal was still in place. Beside it crouched a woman with fair, ragged looking hair hanging down her back. In her hand was a polythene wrap of chrysanthemums, their blooms tightly clenched. By her side stood a large, filthy and bulging wheelie shopping bag. A wrap of dead flowers lay on the cover. She turned her head. Her skin and complexion were rough and weather-worn, lips chapped, grey eyes feral and mistrusting. James ran past her. After a second or two he looked back. She had left the fresh flowers beside the notice and was walking slowly in the same direction as he was, pulling the bag behind her.

James was moved by the sight of her. He had no notion of how it must be to live a homeless and nomadic life in London, or anywhere else for that matter, and could only imagine that it was such an uncomfortable and uncertain existence as to cause its unfortunate victims, for that is how he considered the homeless, to be thoroughly different from normal, civilised, human beings in almost every respect. And yet, he marvelled to himself, small acts of kindness were common to all mankind and that poor woman had wanted to pay her respects.

He ran a short circuit around the park and back onto the canal path. As he approached the witness appeal he could see that a man and a woman were beside it. The woman bent down to look at the flowers. Neither of them was dressed for a stroll along the canal. He was wearing a jacket and trousers. She, a suit. Police. James could just tell. He slowed down as he drew nearer, recognised them, and stopped.

"Hello again," he said and, cocking his head towards the flowers, added cheerily, "Just delivered."

Malek turned to look at him. "Mr Mitchell," he deadballed back.

His flat tone suggested that James's jest had mildly irritated him. James caught the inflection and considered apologising and running on, but he understood the feeling of wanting to just get a job done while others around you are being flippant, and felt that he should try to be helpful.

"I saw a woman put them there, must have been twenty or twenty-five minutes ago."

Malek exchanged a rapid glance with his partner and asked, "Can you describe the person who placed the flowers there?"

James did his best. "Female, couldn't tell her age, thin, fair-haired, messy. Possibly dreadlocks, I wasn't taking that much notice. She looked homeless, if you know what I mean? Scruffy. She had a wheelie bag with her. She went that way." He pointed back towards the zoo. "Can't have been more than about half an hour ago at the most. Twenty minutes more like."

Sanders turned to Malek and spoke urgently. "I'll catch her up. You take the car. Go beyond where she can have got to, get on the path and then walk back. One of us should see her. Where do you reckon you should go? Shit, she'll have to leave the canal at Islington. The path doesn't go through the tunnel."

She turned to James. "Was she walking fast, sir?"

James thought back to the woman's gradual progress. "Definitely not."

Sanders turned back to Malek. "OK. To be on the safe side start at Chapel Market. Go down to Muriel Street through the housing estate off Barnsbury Road and get on the canal there, you know?"

Malek did know. Sanders was already jogging on the spot.

"Go there, then walk back up the canal this way. If she's still on it, she can't have got further than that."

She turned to run.

Malek was uncertain. "But she might not still be on the canal. She could have gone anywhere."

Sanders's look was derisive. "Got a better idea then?"

She waited a fraction of a second then set off at an impressive sprint. Malek turned to James and resisted the urge to roll his eyes.

"Thank you again, Mr Mitchell. If necessary, we will ring and ask you to make a statement about this." He set off at a heavy jog back to his car. He wasn't built for running.

WEST HADDON

MID MORNING

Tebbutt and Edwards, or whatever they were called, struck Patrick as decent coppers. They listened attentively as Charlie made the clearly painful effort to recall how the accident had occurred. Their questions were fair and open ended. Patrick did not need to intervene.

Charlie admitted that he had been tired. He had not slept since the night before but had drunk a lot of coffee during the evening and had kept himself awake on the journey with Red Bull and loud music. Rob had driven for the first half hour and then Charlie had taken over as his brother slept. Just south of Northampton, Charlie had decided to turn off the M1 onto A- and B-roads as he thought the extra concentration required would help keep him awake. He did not believe he was travelling at excessive speed, although it was true to say that he wanted to get home as soon as possible.

Patrick noted that the police did not press Charlie on that point. Tyre marks at the scene of an accident are usually a more reliable indicator of a vehicle's speed than the driver's estimate. As for the motorcycle, Charlie said it had seemed that it had come from nowhere. He could give no reason for not having stopped at the junction but had to accept that he might have fallen asleep. He could not say whether or not his brother was awake when the bike hit them. He remembered the impact and losing of control of the car. He would never forget his brother's screams. He was deeply sorry.

When the constables were satisfied that everything had been covered they concluded the interview, extracted the three separate CDs from the recorder, sealed and taped them. Then Patrick, Charlie and both constables signed each pack.

Patrick knew that there was no point asking what offence Charlie would be charged with. The file would be passed to the CPS for that decision.Pulling out of a junction would be covered by careless driving. The penalty for that could be a fine and disqualification from driving with relief all round. But Patrick's assessment was that realistically Charlie was likely to be charged with the more serious offence of causing injury by dangerous driving. By his own account he had failed to observe the road signs leading up to the junction, and the junction itself, not to mention the motorcycle. The maximum penalty was a five-year prison sentence. Charlie's best hope was for a suspended sentence. Patrick would have to think carefully about who in Chambers would be the best person to represent him.

Anthea had collected the dogs by the time the police left so they were able to depart without incident. Charlie ran his hands through his hair.

"Thank fuck that's over. Can we go and see Rob, Dad? Would that be OK?"

In the car, Charlie was more talkative than he had been for days.

"You know you told me to tell the truth Dad, and that that was the most important thing, yeah?"

Patrick nodded.

"Well, I can see that it's important when the police are involved, like with me. But I was thinking, is the truth always the most important thing? I mean, what if, just say, someone asks you a question. You know that if you tell the truth they could be really hurt, or might pass it on to someone else who really shouldn't know about it. Should you still tell the truth?"

Patrick considered.

"Normally, I would say yes. I would say that if someone asks me a question there would be no point me answering at all if I wasn't going to tell the truth. I think responsibility lies with the person who asks the question. They have to be very careful before they ask it and consider how they might feel if they don't get the answer they want."

He rather hoped that Charlie would leave it at that but Charlie's thoughts progressed.

"Does that let everyone else just do what they like and blame anyone who calls them out on it for asking the question?"

Patrick knew the answer. He just was not very good at applying it to himself.

"By no means. It means that everyone else has to behave in a way that means they are comfortable with telling the truth, if they are called to account. Shall we have the radio on?" He reached forward to press the knob on the dashboard. Rachmaninov. The third piano concerto, a stirring and emotive piece but it fell impotently short of the target of distracting Charlie from his theme.

"Or what about at work then, right? Say I've got a vendor who's moving house because they live next door to the neighbours from hell. A prospective purchaser rings up and asks what the neighbours are like? What do I say?"

Patrick considered. "It's a tricky one because you don't know the truth there. They may not be the neighbours from hell. The vendor may be the problem. I think you'd be OK to fudge that one."

"Even though what I've been told is that the neighbours are awful."

"Well yes, because, as I say, they may be OK. If the prospective purchaser asks what the vendor thinks of the neighbours, then you tell them, but they probably wouldn't put the question that way, would they?"

Charlie was silent for a moment.

"OK, so here's another scenario, right. What if, say, Mum asked you if you were having an affair, and you were, you'd admit it then, would you?"

Patrick was not enjoying this train of thought. "According to my original theory, yes."

"Wow." Charlie sat back. Then another thought burst forth. "But she might not want to know, really."

"Then she shouldn't ask. Charlie where is this all coming from?"

They were approaching Oxford. Patrick would have liked to have speeded up a bit but the traffic was heavy so he had to crawl along on the outskirts of the city as Charlie continued his idle thoughts.

"Nowhere really. It was just you saying that the truth is the most important thing. Because at first you think yes, obviously it is. But there are other things too, aren't there, like hurting people's feelings. That's all I was thinking. And actually —"

Patrick waited for another broadside.

"Even with me. Just say the motorcyclist had died or couldn't remember anything, and there were no witnesses, and Rob had been asleep, so I was the only person who knew what happened, right? So, I could basically say what I liked when the police asked me what happened. If I said a bird hit the car or a deer or something and made out it was totally not my fault, wouldn't everyone be happier because then there wouldn't be all the blame and worry?"

"I think you're asking the wrong person Charlie. Or, maybe the right person, I don't know, but in my experience, professionally I mean, I would say that sooner or later the truth usually gets out, so you're better off telling it at the start. Of course it doesn't always, but a liar doesn't always find it easy to live with himself, or herself."

"So, I'll tell Mum to ask you about your affair then, shall I?"

Patrick turned to him. "What?!"

Charlie laughed. "Ha! Got you there, Dad! Watch out!"

They were approaching a zebra crossing. A woman had stepped onto it. Patrick braked hard and she walked across without acknowledgement.

Charlie's mind was still elsewhere.

"Cos also, I mean about telling the truth and everything. I mean obviously joking about Mum, but it's a good point because what about when someone should know about something but they don't ask. What then, Dad? Do you tell them or not?"

Patrick sensed that this was no longer a casual enquiry.

"It depends, Charlie, doesn't it? Can you think of an example?"

Charlie was silent. Patrick indicated to turn into the hospital car park. As he pulled into a space, Charlie's voice was small.

"Rob didn't want us to drive home on Friday night, Dad. It was my idea. I made him. If we hadn't left when we did, this wouldn't have happened. I didn't tell the police that."

Patrick had rarely before felt the burden of fatherhood bear down on him so heavily. He summoned every persuasive argument he could find to ease his son's troubled mind.

"Charlie, you can't do this to yourself. Whether you had left then or at some different time is not what caused the accident. The police didn't need to know that."

"No, what caused the accident was me not paying enough attention. It's my fault, Dad, whichever way we look at it, and yet I can't even be the one who is badly injured."

"Don't you think so, Charlie? Don't you think that the mental anguish you are suffering is every bit as bad as what Rob's going through, because I do. My boy, listen to me. Bad things happen. But you deciding to drive home when you did was certainly not the cause of this accident. We don't know what it was. But that was not. We don't know anything about how fast the motorbike was going or where it was in the road. We don't know what the driver was doing. There are a whole range of possibilities and one of them is that, at the moment of impact, your car's position in the road might actually have saved Rob's life. On the other hand it might be that yes, you missing the junction was the sole cause of the accident, but, from what you said this morning, I doubt that. The fact is that we simply don't know. But what we do both know is that you can't change what has happened, Charlie. But this is important: very often when something goes wrong people are judged on what they do next and the fact that now, right now, you are supporting Mum and me and Rob and you've told the police everything they need to know is the very best and the only thing you can do now and I am proud of you."

Patrick had no idea if his words had made any impact. But Charlie had no more questions.

They found Jenny in the relatives' room. She didn't smile.

"I couldn't disturb you. Look, Rob's OK but they've discovered that his wound is infected. He had a temperature this morning and, well anyway, they could open him up again but they really don't want to have to do that, obviously. He's had a CT scan and there's an abscess. As soon as they can, they're going to try and drain it. But if they can't, they'll have to operate again. So we have to wait to hear." She shrugged, helplessly.

Charlie looked to each of his parents in turn. "I'll go and get drinks, shall I?"

REGENT'S CANAL

AROUND MIDDAY

Running in work clothes was thoroughly unenjoyable. Jayne's tights gave no purchase on the soles of her brogues and caused her toes to slip and thud against the leather at every footfall. Her waist and thighs were constricted by a lack of give in her trousers while her jacket flapped annoyingly around her sides and felt tight and wet with perspiration under her arms. It was not possible to settle into a regular pace because she was forced to slow down to look sideways at any benches occupied by more than one person and along pathways off the canal for someone who matched the meagre description she had to work on. She was forced to weave in and out of walkers, joggers and cyclists and lost precious seconds leaving and then rejoining the canal at Camden Lock which was crowded with strolling sightseers and shoppers. Nevertheless, Jayne kept running, clinging to the theory that soon enough she would catch up with the woman who, by her calculation, was only moving at half her pace.

She passed beneath bridges, each one different from the others in design and material. Some were sturdy, Victorian structures, others more functional and metal along which trains rumbled and screeched and beneath which her footsteps echoed delightfully. Yellow-brown brick walls which lined sections of her route were landmarked by graffiti. She caught whiffs of cooking from she knew not where and of ice cream as she passed mothers with young children, and snatches of conversation, many in foreign languages, those in English almost all about food or property. And she scarcely noticed the heritage that lay along her route: warehouses, ironmongery and concrete slopes rising from the water which had been built for the convenience of nineteenth century horses who regularly fell in.

With her mind and focus fixed on her goal, she ignored brightly coloured narrow boats and floating cruisers moored along the way as she drew on the muscle memory of circuits she had done as a schoolgirl and pounded forward. She urged herself to keep going as the pain in her feet, now blistered as well as bruised, cried out to stop.

JOHN RADCLIFFE HOSPITAL

MIDDAY

They had spent so many hours sitting in these stiff chairs that each of them had adopted a usual seat. Charlie sat by the window reading the newspaper he had picked up in the shop. Jenny occupied the chair nearest the door, anxiously fidgeting with a piece of loose skin beside her thumbnail and looking up at every new sound. Patrick was opposite her, crossing and recrossing his legs beside the leaflet rack.

"Gracia Peel's getting divorced," Charlie announced. "I didn't know she was married."

"Who?" Jenny replied.

"Gracia Peel. The actress? She was in a thing called *Initiate* about paedophiles on Netflix. You probably didn't watch it."

Patrick affected interest with disinterest. "Gracia Peel? I'm sure I've heard of her."

"Blonde. Little. Attractive. Blue eyes. She's got a kind of vulnerability about her." That was Charlie's take on Gracia. "Look." He proffered the newspaper to his mother. Jenny perused it for the agony of thirty seconds while Patrick sustained a detached air.

"Oh dear," said Jenny. "Sounds like her husband has been up to no good." Patrick could barely restrain himself from snatching the newspaper.

Jenny continued to muse. "Yes, I see what you mean about her being attractive. What do you think, Patrick?" She passed the paper to him.

At last.

A quarter page portrait of Gracia, looking grave yet beautiful in a printed top over tight jeans sat below the headline,

GRACIA SAYS "IT'S OVER!"

Following this paper's revelations of allegations that British actress, Gracia Peel's husband Claudio Benettini took part in a sex romp in Rome earlier this month, a representative of Gracia Peel has announced that the couple are to divorce.

Peel married Benettini, a travel journalist, in a private ceremony in Bellagio in 2015. The couple have lived privately, dividing their lives between Italy and the UK. They have no children.

Gracia Peel is best known for her portrayal of Annie in *Initiate* (2017). Filming of the second series is due to start in the summer with release expected in 2020. Her statement read "Gracia Peel is very sad to announce that she and her husband have decided to separate. She asks for privacy at this difficult time." Claudio Benettini was unavailable for comment.

Patrick looked closer at the image of Gracia. The print on her blouse represented haloed angels.

"Hot, don't you think, Dad?" Charlie asked.

"If you say so." Patrick handed the paper back to Charlie.

"Oh come on, Dad. She's hot. Admit it," Charlie persisted.

Something snapped.

"Leave it Charlie. I'm really not interested in actresses at the moment, hot or otherwise."

Charlie looked desolate. "Sorry, I wasn't thinking."

Jenny shook her head. "It's all right, love. We're all still a bit worried about Rob, that's all."

Patrick stood up.

"I'm going outside to make a call."

Jenny looked concerned.

"You can do it here, can't you?"

He shook his head. "I'll go outside."

At the smoking area two pony-tailed girls in leggings were standing beside a young male patient seated in a wheelchair who looked to be not much older than they were. He was wearing a dressing gown, pyjamas and slippers. Beside him was a metal pole on wheels with a drip attached. All three were pulling deeply on cigarettes. Patrick stood a few yards away and dialled Islington Police Station. He was put through to Malek's voicemail.

"Hello, it is Patrick Kingdom here. I was supposed to come in to see you this afternoon. I am afraid I am going to have to postpone my visit. My son is very ill in hospital. I do apologise. Goodbye."

A text arrived as soon as he hung up. It was from Jenny.

Come back. Doctor here.

REGENT'S CANAL

A LITTLE LATER

Jayne was almost at St Pancras Basin. Worry that the woman had deviated from the path had begun to weigh heavily and diminish her resolve to continue. What was the point? She didn't want to have to run all the way to Limehouse Basin. Then she remembered that, sooner or later, she would meet Jalal walking the other way from Islington. So long as their target stayed on the path, one or other of them would see her. If they did not, then at least they could rule out one explanation for her whereabouts, and what else did they have to go on? Doubt allayed, she refocused her mind towards her goal and quickened her steps.

The canal swung round a wide curve at Gasholder Park where massive iron structures which had been constructed in the nineteenth century to store gas had been converted into circular apartment blocks. Half a dozen surrounded a grassy playground which was ringed by the skeleton of one gasholder. The area was clean and gentrified and furnished with benches. Suddenly, there it was.

At the far end of the bend she spotted a wheelie bag standing next to a bench on which a man and a woman were seated either side of two cans of cider. Everything about their appearance distinguished them from conventional society. Their clothes were grubby and indistinct. The man's hair hung shaggily around his weatherworn face. The woman was leaning forward, her head supported by her hands. Her fingernails and cuticles were ingrained with dirt, wrists circled by grimy sleeve cuffs. Matted clumps of yellow hair hung from her head and along her back. Jayne stopped running, took a second and said to her, "Excuse me."

The woman did not respond. The man looked to Jayne.

"Is that her bag?" she repeated, forced to look at the man.

"Who is asking?" he replied.

She produced her warrant card. "Police. Can you tell me if that bag is hers?" The woman had not moved. The man touched her gently on the shoulder. "Police, Rosie." It was a clear warning.

Jayne spoke carefully. "Listen, please don't worry. You're doing nothing wrong. I'm just making enquiries into an incident which occurred on the canal near Regent's Park earlier this month."

The woman looked towards the man who sighed and turned his head away. Her grey eyes returned to Jayne.

"Talking about Davey, are you?" Irish accent. Jayne nodded.

"David McBrain. Yes."

The expression in the woman's eyes was dull and unreadable. Jayne wondered if it might be fatigue, or if she was sick or withdrawing from a drug. All three were likely. Much later on in the day she would understand. The woman was suffering from profound grief.

JOHN RADCLIFFE HOSPITAL, OXFORD

LATE AFTERNOON

The medics could not explain how Rob's wound had become infected. The likeliest explanation was that the infection had been produced internally. It didn't matter now. A radiologist had successfully drained the abscess with the careful and precise use of instruments and imaging. There was no need for further surgery and Rob's recovery could continue. It had been another emotionally draining wait. None of them was sure how many more they could take.

ISLINGTON POLICE STATION

LATE AFTERNOON

Jalal had found Rosie Sheehan sitting with Jayne beside the canal at Gasholder Park. To his surprise, she had agreed to accompany them to the station to make a statement. They seated her in an interview room where, with the edges of a misshapen cardigan criss-crossed over her chest and clutched together by grimy fingers which protruded from ragged fingerless gloves, she had begun to answer their questions. She was a poor storyteller. She dwelt on irrelevant and insignificant detail, then lapsed into tear-drenched silences from which she would revive with a barrage of questions concerning what had happened to Davey McBrain and how he could have just disappeared.

Animated one minute, exhausted the next, she had subsided into weeping and spent inarticulacy. They offered tea, water, a cigarette break, whatever she needed.

"I just need to sleep," she had said, at which point Jalal and Jayne had agreed that they needed to pause the interview.

"Miss Sheehan, may we call you Rosie?" Jayne had enquired.

"Suppose."

"Rosie, we don't have bedrooms here, only cells. You can sleep if you need to, but it will have to be in a cell."

"That will do. I'm not in the habit of sleeping on a mattress."

Back at her desk, Jayne rolled her eyes.

"What's she up to Jal? I thought she was going to co-operate. Not so sure now. She's not just come for in for a kip, has she?"

Jalal considered. "I don't know."

But what do we know so far? Jayne continued. "David McBrain was her lover, ex-Army. Obviously had a few mental health problems." Jayne swept the aborted statement with the back of her hand. "Wasn't the only one, was he? That's about it, isn't it? Know what I mean?"

Jalal spoke. "This isn't a mental health thing, is it? But you're right, she obviously did love the bloke. That's the point, isn't it? She wants to know what happened. We've got to give her the benefit of the doubt, haven't we? He paused to think. "Listen, how about when she wakes up, you carry on without me. She may feel more comfortable that way."

Jayne looked surprised. "Are you sure?"

He smiled. "Sure. You've got this."

ISLINGTON POLICE STATION

8:00pm

Jayne waited impatiently for Jalal to answer his phone. It rang three times then he answered. Her voice was urgent.

"Jal, are you at home?"

"Yes."

"By a laptop?"

"Yes."

"OK hold on I'm going to email you something. Ring me when you've read it." She could barely contain herself.

Ten minutes later Jalal rang back.

"How did you manage that?"

Jayne tried to sound casual. "Chocolate. It turns out that Rosie Sheehan runs on chocolate. She woke up, said she was hungry and I thought 'here we go'. So we gave her the room service menu which, as you know, is a little limited, but it does include chocolate and once she'd got a couple of Mars bar inside her, she was off like a dog on a racetrack, focused, coherent .. well, see for yourself."

"And do you believe her?"

"Absolutely."

"We need to speak to the pathologist."

Jayne contradicted him. "Done that."

"Does it add up?"

Jayne smiled at him. A glorious, triumphant smile. "It adds up, Jal."

WEDNESDAY 24th APRIL

WEST HADDON

8:00am

"Shall I make one for you?"

Jenny stood at the island piling ham and cheese onto buttered bread for Charlie's sandwiches.

Patrick was on his way through the kitchen to the car. "No, thanks. I'll be fine. Keep me in touch."

He caught the train from Rugby and went into Chambers. The head criminal clerk listened sympathetically to his news and assured him that he could be absent for as long as necessary. Patrick wasn't due in court for a couple of weeks. They agreed that if he would sort out which files and papers from his room he needed at home they could be couriered there tomorrow.

On the train he had texted Gray suggesting lunch at Middle Temple. Gray had replied.

Yes. 1:15pm fine. G.

JOHN RADCLIFFE HOSPITAL, OXFORD

DAYTIME

As Jenny had expected, Charlie insisted on accompanying her to the hospital. She had hoped that yesterday's news would lift his spirits but the impression she gained was that he intended to suffer for as long as his brother did.

Rob was conscious but very tired and he slept for long periods. Charlie was unsettled. He frequently found reasons to go for a wander, despite Jenny's insistence that the tea from the cafe was virtually undrinkable, thus denying him one avenue of distraction. Instead he would sit for a while, then get up, go to the shop, return with a newspaper or book of puzzles that he would subsequently be unable to concentrate on. Periodically, he would just look with concern at his brother. Quite apart from the internal injuries, there was Rob's hip and pelvis to worry over. The news was that they would heal but the process would be long, frustrating and difficult.

Jenny was content to sit quietly beside Rob's bed. Her mind was at its easiest when she was close to him. She had plenty of time to look around her. Other patients came and went. She suspected that the strained and anxious expressions of their relatives reflected her own. Today there was a new patient across the ward. All she could see was a large frame covering the lower half of the body. A woman of her own age was seated on the chair beside the bed, leaning forward. When their eyes met briefly, Jenny smiled in the hope of giving comfort. The woman appeared to make a brave effort to smile back.

It was easy to lose track of time. At some point, Charlie said he fancied going to get a paper and she decided to go with him. In the corridor they passed the same woman. She stopped and spoke.

"Hello, saw you in there. Needed a breather?"

Jenny smiled, "Yes."

The woman seemed to want to chat. "Is it your son, you're with?"

"Yes. How about you?"

The woman nodded. "Road accident last week. He was doing all right, but something's gone wrong. They are worried he might lose his leg."

Jenny felt helpless. She didn't realise that simply being able to tell someone else about her son's condition was a small comfort to the other mother.

"Oh, I'm so sorry."

"Is yours going to be all right?"

Jenny shrugged. "We hope so, but in here you never really know do you?"

Charlie had been standing aside, letting the two mothers speak. "Car crash?" he asked.

The woman turned to him. "Sort of. He was on his motorbike. A car just pulled out in front of him. But it was my fault cos I'd tidied away his high vis jacket." Her chin puckered as she shook her head. "He could have died."

Then she pulled back her shoulders, "No, I must be strong. You have to be, don't you?" She looked at Charlie's sling. "Looks like you've been in the wars too."

Charlie acknowledged the comment with the smallest possible movement of his head and turned away.

The woman reached out to Jenny's arm and gave it a squeeze. "Stay brave."

Charlie sat in silence for the rest of the afternoon. From time to time he looked over to the bed opposite them. At one point a group of doctors gathered and the nurse pulled the curtains around them. Charlie looked at Jenny then lowered his head. When the curtains were pulled aside, he looked back. The woman caught the interest in his eye and stood up. She walked over to them, smiling.

"Might be able to save the leg, they say. He's going to be OK." She sighed and patted her chest. Two wells of tears flooded her eyes. "God! I wasn't expecting that."

She looked down at Rob then turned to Jenny and spoke kindly. "I hope he's OK. This is no place for a young man."

She put a hand on Jenny's shoulder and returned to her vigil. Jenny looked to Charlie.

"She said he's going to be OK, Charlie. That's what she said, OK?"

ISLINGTON POLICE STATION

11:00am

CONFIDENTIAL
WITNESS STATEMENT

Criminal Justice Act 1967, Section 9, Magistrates Court Act 180, sub section 5A (3)(a) and 5B,Criminal Procedure Rules 2005, Rule 27.1

Statement of ROSIE MARIE SHEEHAN

Age if under 18: Over 18 (if over 18 insert 'over 18')
Occupation: Unemployed

This statement (consisting of 2 pages each signed by me) is true to the best of my knowledge and belief and I make it knowing that, if it is tendered in evidence, I shall be liable to prosecution if I have wilfully stated in it anything which I know to be false or do not believe to be true.

Dated the 23rd day of April 2019

My name is Rosie Marie Sheehan. I am 30 years old. I was born in Belfast. I have no permanent address. I sleep at various locations in London. Nowadays it is usually near King's Cross or somewhere in town but occasionally I go to Bridge No. 9 on the Regent's Canal because it is quiet there.

Just over a year ago I met Davey McBrain. He was born in Belfast too. His lifestyle was similar to mine. We formed a relationship.

Davey told me that he had moved to England as a child with his parents and that when he left school he joined the Army. He did a tour of duty in Afghanistan and was discharged with post traumatic stress disorder. He got a job as a night time security officer. Davey was married then but he had no children. He found out that his wife was having an affair. He attacked the other man and was sentenced to a term of eight years imprisonment. In prison he became addicted to spice. His wife divorced him. I am not sure when he came out of prison but I know that he has had nowhere permanent to live for at least eighteen months. He told me he was still on licence.

WHAT LIES BENEATH THE SURFACE

Davey and I spent the night of April 3rd 2019 to April 4th 2019 near to King's Cross. I told him that I was not going to be around during the day on April 4th and to meet me at Bridge No. 9, near London Zoo that evening.

April 5th was his birthday. My idea was that we would walk to the zoo and look at the birds and animals that we could see from the canal bridge and the road by the zoo. I do not think Davey had ever done that before. To my knowledge he was not familiar with that part of the canal.

At some time during the evening of April 4th I walked along the canal path to meet Davey. I found him lying on the ground. He had a bad injury to his wrist and a cut and a bruise on the side of his head, near the front. He did not complain of a cut on the back of his head and I did not see one.

He was conscious and breathing. He said he had had a bit to drink and a smoke. He told me that he had mistaken another woman on the canal for me. She had been with a man who had kissed her. Davey said that he had felt angry with the man and had hit him to try to get him away from the woman who he thought was me. The man had pushed him in the stomach and Davey had fallen over. He said he had landed on his wrist and bumped his head a bit. He did not know who the man was or who the woman was. He fell asleep beside the canal. When I arrived he got up and we walked to Bridge No. 9, close by. Davey's wrist was very painful but he did not want to go to hospital. I do not believe he was suffering from concussion or any other ill effects of his fall. We spent the night there together. We drank some cider and had a couple of smokes (spice). I told Davey he should go somewhere else because the man he hit might go to the police and Davey would be at risk of being returned to prison, under the terms of his licence. Davey said we should sleep first and that he would go after that.

When I woke up it was very dark. I do not know what the time was but Davey was no longer there. I looked around for him but I could not see him. I guessed that he had gone back down to King's Cross or maybe even further down the canal because there are other places to sleep there.

I packed my bag and followed him. During the next few days I walked a long way down the canal asking if anyone had seen Davey. Nobody had seen him since April 2nd.

I think it was about three days later that I returned to Bridge No. 9. I was informed that Davey's body had been found in the canal early in the morning of April 5th.

I have no explanation for how Davey died. I loved him very much and we had never had an argument or fight. He has never expressed any suicidal thoughts.

When I returned to Bridge No. 9 I saw that a police sign asking for witnesses had been placed on the path. I did not contact the police because I could not explain how Davey's body was in the canal or how he had died.

I put flowers beside the sign and have been staying nearby ever since in the hope that I might hear an explanation for Davey's death. Approximately a week ago a policeman came to the bridge and showed me a photograph of Davey. He told me that he was investigating Davey's death. I now know that that was DC Jalal Malek. Today I decided to leave the area so I replaced the flowers and began to walk back to King's Cross. I have with me some of Davey's possessions that he left beside the bridge.

I do not know if Davey could swim.

While I was walking towards King's Cross this morning I was apprehended by DC Jayne Sanders.

Signed *Rosie Sheehan*   **Dated** *23 April 2019*

Jayne placed Rosie's statement with the others in the file beneath the document which set out the conclusions that she and Jalal had reached. The word around the station was that Cartwright was in a filthy mood. It was rumoured that he had been placed on a diet by his wife following the excesses of Easter and accordingly his blood sugar level was low.

Cartwright called her and Jalal into his office. Jayne placed the file neatly before him next to the cup of coffee, which she observed was black. There was no sign of a bun. In each corner of his mouth were white gobbets of undiluted mucus which stretched elastically as he spoke. He thanked them for their work over the weekend and asked for a summary of the evidence, which Jalal gave.

Cartwright observed that Rosie Sheehan was clearly a significant witness. He asked whether it was their belief that she was truthful or whether they thought she had been responsible for McBrain's death.

Jayne replied. "We do not believe she is responsible, sir. no. Rosie Sheehan is grieving. She does not appear to have either the intelligence or intention to cover up how McBrain died. It is our belief that, if she had been responsible for his death, she would not have admitted to having found him alive on the evening of April 4th, nor indeed to having known him or even having been there at any time that evening. She appears to be as concerned as we are to find out how he died. As for whether or not she is truthful, I think the only matter on which she was possibly not one hundred per cent reliable was the amount of drugs and drink she said that she and McBrain had taken. She gave several estimates. They were all very low by comparison with the levels found post-mortem in Mr McBrain's body. Since her estimations of the quantity of drugs taken was variable, they are omitted from her statement."

Cartwright probed further.

"But do you believe her when she says that McBrain was alive and relatively well when she found him?"

"We do sir. We can think of no reason why she would say otherwise." She looked to Jalal. He stood squarely before the DS, head up.

Cartwright addressed him.

"DC Malek have you drawn any conclusion as to how Mr McBrain might have died then?"

Jalal looked briefly at Jayne, then spoke. "We believe it was an accident, sir."

Cartwright's eyebrows raised.

"An accident? Go on."

"The water is not deep in that section of canal. The bottom is muddy and rough, strewn with objects including pieces of rock and concrete. The path beside the canal is constructed of blue brick edged with concrete kerbstones. It is mostly level and well maintained but in some places, including areas close to where the deceased's body was found, the bricks are raised and uneven and the kerb stones are broken. There are photographs, sir. Coincidentally, the witness James Mitchell referred to the woman he met with Patrick Kingdom tripping on one of the paving bricks that same evening."

Cartwright nodded.

"Contrary to Rosie Sheehan's initial assumption, we do not believe that Mr McBrain left Bridge No. 9 during the night of 4th to 5th April with the intention of leaving permanently since his belongings were all left beneath the bridge. However, we do know that he got up during the night, before Rosie Sheehan woke up. Rosie Sheehan observed that it was not yet light when she awoke, and that he was no longer with her. It will have been very dark. There are no lights on the canal. There was heavy cloud. It is reasonable to assume that Mr McBrain was disorientated, given his unfamiliarity with his surroundings combined with the effect of drink and drugs."

Cartwright remained silent. Jalal pressed on.

"Sir, if you turn to the pathologist's report you will see that he found a cut on the back of the deceased's head. There is no bruising around it. Rosie Sheehan does not mention that he had a cut on the back of his head when she first encountered him on the canal. She only mentions a cut on the side of his head, near to the front. We pressed her on that matter and she said that she did not see one on the back of his head, neither did he complain of one. But there was definitely a cut on the back of his head when he died. Its position is consistent with Mr McBrain having struck his head on a hard object lying on the bottom of the canal.

Cartwright's reaction was still unreadable. Jalal continued.

"It is our conclusion that he got up in the night in the condition described, and unwittingly walked too close to the canal. He tripped, probably stumbled, and fell in, hit his head, fell unconscious and drowned before any bruising began to form around the cut. We cannot know whether there was bleeding from the cut as any blood will have been washed away by the water. Nevertheless, we have spoken to the pathologist this morning, sir. He says that our conclusion is logical and consistent with his findings. Naturally we considered the possibility that he had had an encounter with another person in the night but there is no evidence to support that theory."

The DS looked up. Jalal had not finished.

"In our minds there is one outstanding matter, sir and that is how Mr McBrain came to have a broken wrist. Rosie Sheehan says that he told her he had a fight with someone who was kissing a woman who looked a little like her. We do wonder if this was Patrick Kingdom, sir, and that the woman he was with was Gracia Peel since she, like Rosie Sheehan, is a naturally fair-haired woman. There is also the possibility that the other witness, James Mitchell might have seen more than he has stated. All of that, however, is speculation and not borne out by any evidence. But it is our conclusion that the possibility that Mr Kingdom and Miss Peel, possibly Mr Mitchell also, might not have been wholly truthful justified our initial line of enquiry."

Jalal paused just briefly enough to ensure that his point had hit home. The DS remained unresponsive. He merely pinched the sides of his mouth and licked his thumb, Jalal continued.

"If our final conclusion is accurate, the injury to Mr McBrain's wrist is unconnected with his death, which, as I say, we conclude was an accident."

Cartwright looked from one to the other. The two DCs had impressed him. They had done sterling work and their findings were logical, flawless and, importantly, saved the need for and expense of further enquiry. He ought to have shown that he was impressed but, he couldn't help it, he was mean spirited, and disinclined to bestow praise.

"So I was right. The answer lay on the tow path, just as I suspected. You'll learn. But, fair's fair, your findings appear sound and I will present them to DI Fraser with my recommendation that they be passed on to the Coroner and the police investigation be closed. There are no next of kin?" He looked at them interrogatively.

"None that Miss Sheehan was aware of, sir."

"Well, let Miss Sheehan know. And all those other people you've been after before they sue us. Start at the top. Thank you. Dismissed."

***

Jayne wanted to punch the air. Once clear of the DS's office, she did. She high-fived Jalal and walked confidently towards her desk. It was piled with CCTV tapes that she had yet to go through.

"Hoo-ray!" She cried jubilantly. "No more CCTV to watch." And with a flourish she launched the pile into a box for disposal.

One was marked "Culworth Street 5.30 to 7.30pm Thursday 4 April 2019". Culworth Street runs along the side of North Gate Mansions. The recording showed Gracia arrive at the entrance to North Gate Mansions shortly after 6.00pm and then leave with Patrick and walk with him towards the canal path an hour later.

MIDDLE TEMPLE HALL

1:30pm

Patrick was sombre as he recounted his family's ordeal. Obviously Rob caused the gravest concern but, provided there were no more setbacks, and there could be many, he was set on a slow journey toward recovery. Jenny was holding up but Charlie's mental health was concerning. Gray had no words beyond offers of support and friendship and an objective appraisal that, given everything that Patrick had told him, they would actually all get through this.

"But," Gray smiled, "I assume you've heard? It seems the police have discovered how your assailant died."

Patrick did not smile back. "So it appears. They called me this morning. I gather the death is no longer being treated as suspicious. I wasn't told why. Doesn't matter really, I suppose. But how do you know?"

"They came to see me yesterday. You see, Gracia had told them that she had spent that evening with me. They wanted corroboration, I imagine."

"Christ!" Patrick was visibly shocked. "What did you say?"

Gray described his interview with Malek, its premature ending and the message he had received that morning which conveyed that the police would not intrude further upon his time.

"So, do we know what happened?" Patrick asked.

"No. We don't. It seems that it is not our business," Gray responded. "I think we should be thankful for that, don't you? I expect it'll all come out at the inquest."

They were seated at either side of a refectory table at the far end of the famously barrel-vaulted hall. Patrick's back was to the panelled wall and he was able to look out at the dark-suited men and women who were taking lunch surrounded by large portraits of ancient eminences.

"Oh no." he said quietly, then more brightly. "Hello."

James Mitchell had approached. Patrick introduced him to Gray. "Do you know each other? James Mitchell. Graham Andrew?"

"Of course. Good afternoon, Judge," replied James, inclining his head toward Gray in obsequious greeting.

Gray attempted an acknowledgement without revealing that he had no recollection of ever having met the man who had intruded upon their conversation.

"Mind if I sit down a minute?" James sat alongside Patrick. "Sorry to interrupt but I was going to ring you later. Bit of news about that canal business."

Patrick gave not a hint of encouragement for James to continue. Nevertheless he did.

"I ran past the place yesterday. The police were there again. I don't think they know what they're doing, you know. I told them I'd seen a woman putting flowers down by the witness appeal a bit earlier on and one of them literally set off at a run after her. Crazy! You'd think they'd have got a bit further with the whole thing by now, wouldn't you?"

Patrick raised his eyes. "Well." That was all he said.

James was disappointed. He'd hoped for a minute or two more in order to get on to the Gracia Peel connection. That would be something to impress the family but he sensed that his audience was over. He addressed both of them. "Anyway, sorry to disturb you, Judge, Patrick," and receiving no encouragement to linger, he stood up and backed away.

Patrick apologised.

"Sorry about him. Terrible gossip."

Gray raised his eyebrows knowingly and took a sip of coffee. Patrick continued.

"Does Gracia know that the death is no longer regarded as suspicious?"

Gray put down his cup and sighed. "I don't know. I'm afraid we rather fell out. I haven't seen her since Easter morning."

Patrick took a sip of water and looked around him. Kitchen staff and diners were coming and going, the regular lunchtime chatter of lawyers at large echoed around the walls and vaulted roof space.

"Gray do you have to get back or can we go somewhere quieter?"

They walked outside and found a bench in a peaceful position overlooking the garden.

Patrick leaned forward, resting his elbows on his knees, looking toward the distant Thames, his mind's eye seeing Jenny, the boys, their home, Gracia. He spoke without turning his head to Gray.

"I saw in the newspaper that Gracia is getting divorced. Is she all right?"

Gray shrugged with a grimace of resignation that Gracia had not shared this news with him herself. "I have no idea Patrick. I hope so. But yes, Neil showed me a newspaper report this morning. I'm not sure I would have known otherwise."

There was a moment or two or silence before Patrick spoke again.

"I am not sure I am going to be able to live with all this you know, Gray. I never did tell the police about the attack. I intended to yesterday but I had to stay with Charlie and then go to the hospital. I was going to go in later today. Do you think I still should?"

Gray made a steeple out of his hands and put his two forefingers by his mouth as he considered carefully. By way of reply he asked "Are you in any doubt at all that you are in any way responsible for the man's death?"

Patrick stared into the garden. A blackbird was pulling at a worm in a flower bed.

"He came out of nowhere and threw his fists at me. Gracia was standing right beside me. I pushed him away and he fell over. If I had not found out that he had died some time afterwards, I would have thought that we had had a lucky escape from an unprovoked attack. I simply do not know what happened after that but he was alive and conscious when we left him."

Gray said nothing, allowing his friend time to think aloud.

"But if I go now and tell them about the assault, where does that get anyone? It still doesn't explain how he drowned. It just adds to the mystery. I honestly don't see how my going in to tell them about this helps. Doesn't it just muddy the water, as Gracia said it would all along? And it would involve her, which is what I hoped to avoid throughout. I'd be laying myself open to charges, wasting police time, perverting the course of justice, maybe her too depending on what, if anything, she has said to them already. Maybe I have just got to live with that?"

The blackbird's beak slipped on the worm. It shook its head vigorously and flew away. The worm disappeared underground. Patrick sighed and leant back on the bench, stretching his legs out in front of him. He appeared to have made a decision.

Then he asked a question: "Would she have been willing to back me up, do you think, if it came to it?"

Gray shook his head. "Who knows. She certainly was not minded to on Sunday."

Patrick gave a half laugh. "You know, I envy her in some ways. I doubt she has been conflicted about this at all. But what about you, Gray? What were you going to say if they had asked if she had been with you that evening?"

Gray took a deep breath and straightened the end of his tie over his shirt. "I had to think about that, Patrick. I got myself in a terrible muddle considering all sorts of other things: loyalty to you, my responsibility to Gracia, all that. But in the end it was easy. If asked the question, I would have had to tell the truth. It is all there is. If we create a fantasised history of events that took place as we would have liked them to have done, rather than as they did, then nothing is real. Nothing would have any point at all."

Patrick looked affectionately at his friend.

"You're a good man, Gray. I suppose my dilemma is whether a truth has to be told even when it is not or no longer asked for. Oddly enough, it is something Charlie asked me. I'm not sure I gave him an answer though."

"And your conclusion?"

Patrick slid his wedding ring to his knuckle between thumb and forefinger as he looked down towards the Thames.

"I don't have one. I know that it is selfish to reveal a truth simply to ease one's conscience. On the other hand, living with a lie can actually be no more than simple cowardice, one wanting to have one's cake and eat it, to use the cliché." He considered. "I suppose it depends on the circumstances, and the people involved. Perhaps it is the case that there is a time and a place for the truth. Perhaps also, well, perhaps sometimes it is better to keep one's mouth shut."

Gray inclined his head sideways as he considered the premise, then nodded slowly. Neither man spoke. They were both thinking of Jenny.

Patrick broke the moment. He pulled his feet beneath the bench and smacked his hands flat onto the top of his knees. "Listen, I think I need to go. I'd like to get to the hospital later."

They said goodbye and arranged to meet for dinner soon. Patrick strode briskly toward his Chambers as Gray set off at a more conservative pace up the ancient cobbled lane leading to The Strand. From behind he heard his name. "Gray!" Then footsteps running toward him. He turned to see Patrick holding out his phone. "Look at this."

It was a short video clip. Rob was sitting up in a hospital bed, waving. "Hi Dad." Beneath was a three-lettered message from Jenny.

xxx.

Back at the RCJ Gray was met in the corridor by Neil, who was pacing agitatedly, apparently having been waiting for him.

"All well, Neil?" Gray enquired.

"I hope so, sir. Gracia arrived about five minutes ago. She is in your room."

She was seated at his desk, a vision of loveliness in a lotus flower print dress beneath a denim jacket. Gray greeted her and stood to her side, somewhat awkwardly displaced.

"I'll do it," she announced. "I'll go to the police and tell them I was with Patrick that night, and what happened by the canal."

Gray was astounded. "Why?"

She picked up his pen, scrawled a triangle on the nearest piece of paper and put it down again.

"Because of Rob and so you don't have to lie. It's what Patrick wants me to do, and it's what you want. So I'll do it. What do I do, ring them now or what?"

Gray was not accustomed to feeling panic.

"Gracia, hold on a minute. I think you're going to have to talk to Patrick. Things have changed."

She looked irritated. "Why? I don't want to talk to Patrick. Just tell me what I do. Do I ring Islington police and make an appointment, or tell them over the phone or what?"

Gray was desperate to slow her down.

"Gracia, listen. I'm not sure it matters any more. Haven't the police rung you today?"

"No idea. I've left my phone at home. I've come to use yours. But you said. I'd got to tell them about us being attacked and all that so Patrick isn't in the shit. I don't mind. I'll do it." She fished in her handbag and pulled out a piece of paper on which appeared to be written a number.

"I'm not sure it's what Patrick wants any more."

"It's the truth though, isn't it? Why don't I just ring them?" She reached for the handset to Gray's landine.

Neil appeared at the door, upright and formal. "Sorry to interrupt, sir, but the Lord Chief is on the phone."

Gray turned to Gracia.

"Listen, I'm sorry, it's the Lord Chief Justice. I can't put him off. Don't ring the police. You need to speak to Patrick. You'll have to sort this out with him. Neil, I'm sorry, would you mind if Gracia came into your room for a minute while she locates Patrick Kingdom? She may need to use your phone."

Gracia looked up at him in surprise as he moved towards her.

"I'm sorry, my dear, but would you mind moving. I need to sit at my desk."

SOHO COFFEE CO, THE STRAND

FIFTEEN MINUTES LATER

Gracia was seated alone at a table. Patrick's compelling impulse was to wrap his arms around her, hold and kiss her there and then. Her beauty was breathtaking. Blonde hair fell around her elfin face in lush waves onto her shoulder. Plump, red lips sat in perfect proportion to her pretty nose. He would have liked to read the expression in her eyes but it was hidden behind large dark glasses.

He suppressed his physical impulse and greeted her in a friendly manner, hoping not to push it too far. At first, her response had been hostile. Her replies to "How are you?" were brittle and short. But she had softened gradually, accepted his offer of coffee and enquired after Rob with what he believed was genuine concern. He expressed condolences over her decision to divorce. She merely rolled her eyes.

"But why are we here, Gracia?"

She repeated her intention to go to the police with a full account of what had happened on the evening they had split up.

He had to stop her. But he had begged her to do this, and asked Gray to persuade her to get on board. And now she was willing. But now it was all different. If she were to volunteer now to the police that she had witnessed McBrain assaulting Patrick and been left prostrate on the canal – if she were to tell them of all that, what can of worms would be opened? The lying to the police can of worms, that was what. They would call him in. He would have to admit that he had lied twice or three times, and tell them what had really happened that night. And it would help not one iota with the enquiry into the death of David McBrain, but it would open both him up to charges of perverting the course of justice, which would lead to Jenny and the boys finding out about everything, and had they not had enough? And, potentially, it would lead to the collapse of his practice and God knows what consequences for Gracia, and basically no, this must not happen. Telling the truth had seemed the cleanest way out when Rob's life had been in danger. But that was then, only a few days ago, my God, when his mind had been altered by impending tragedy. He had been wrong. The truth would have ruined everybody's lives and saved nobody's. How the hell was he going to explain this to her now?

He did his best.

She listened. When he finished she looked at him. "I don't get you at all you know. One minute you're saying I've got to tell the police everything, the next I haven't. I mean, fine, whatever. I didn't want to anyway. But I mean, honestly? The whole truth and nothing but, right? That's your business isn't it? I don't know. For a lawyer, you are seriously fucked up, aren't you?" And she swung out, leaving him with a mug of cold froth.

He texted Gray.

Gray. So sorry for disruption. Have spoken to Gracia. She now content to leave everything as is. P.

MANCHESTER SQUARE, MARYLEBONE

EARLY EVENING

Gray read Patrick's text at the end of the afternoon and walked home. It was a warm, pleasant evening. As he shut the front door behind him, the atmosphere within held a different quality from the quiet order which normally prevailed. Sometimes odours of detergent and polish announced that the cleaners had been in during the day. It wasn't that. He put his keys down on the hall table and walked through to the kitchen. A bag of shopping sat on the worktop. Warmth pervaded the air and a pan of water simmered gently on the hob, beside which a bottle of red wine stood open and breathing.

Gracia strolled in from the snug, holding a half full glass. "Hi." she said, "Hungry?"

"Oh hello," he replied, "how nice. Yes, I am actually. Do I have time to change?"

"Course."

Gray went upstairs. He removed his phone from the inside pocket of his jacket and, through force of habit, quickly checked through his emails.

Re: Hello again.
From: Maitland, V.

To: Me
Vanessa.

He sat down to read.

Dear Gray

It was such a nice surprise to see you on Easter Sunday. I am sorry that I could not stay longer and catch up properly.

It was good to see you looking well. I know I have not been in touch but your career has been prominent news in legal circles and I have been privately delighted to see how successful you have been.

My news is different and a longer story than I can tell here. My practice has developed well and I'm pleased to be where I am, doing good quality work. However, any wider ambitions I might have had have been inhibited by the demands of single parenthood. I don't know if you know, but thirteen years ago I married a specialist at Great Ormond Street. Unfortunately the marriage did not last. The boys are still in touch with their father and we try to maintain a pleasant relationship, although there are strains, as you might imagine.

Gray, I want to say this. Seeing you again reminded me of the happy times we spent together. When all was said and done, I think we did enjoy each other's company. So I am taking a bit of a risk here, but I wonder if you might like to meet for dinner one evening, just to catch up, perhaps? Of course, if there is someone in your life who would prefer this not to happen, or if you would prefer to leave things as they are, I completely understand. As I say, I am aware that I'm taking a risk in suggesting this.

Anyway, do let me know.

With my fondest wishes,

Vanessa.

Gray's eyebrows lifted. "Golly!" he said.

He went downstairs. Gracia had poured him a drink. "Mussels," she announced. "Oh. You didn't change."

He looked down at his suit. "Oh. No," he replied vaguely.

"Are you okay?"

"Um, yes. I've just had an email."

Gracia laughed. "Wild!"

"It was from Vanessa."

Gracia looked intrigued. "Really? Are you two still in touch?"

"No, not at all. I haven't heard from her for years."

"What did she want?"

"Well, she's wondering if I'd like to meet up for dinner or something."

"What, just out of the blue?"

"Well not totally, we bumped into one another a few days ago."

"Gosh. Oh. Well, anyway, are you ready to eat?"

They sat down. Gracia tore off two sheets of kitchen roll and passed one to Gray.

"Sorry. I couldn't find any napkins."

The mussels were drenched in oil and garlic. Chunks of warm, crusty bread lay in a basket in the middle of the table. Gracia ladled the clattering contents of the pan onto their plates. The food was welcome and delicious.

Gray waited for her to introduce the inevitable subject of the day's event.

"So. Patrick talked me out of it. He probably told you."

"Only briefly, but he did text me, yes."

"Surprised he didn't send that text to me, with his track record. They had tried to get hold of me actually, the police. They just left a message asking me to ring them back." She wiped her mouth.

"And did you?"

"I did actually. Not till after I'd seen you and Patrick obviously. They just said they had concluded that the bloke had not died in suspicious circumstances and that they would not be troubling me any more. They thanked me actually. I wonder what did happen to him? Do you know?"

"No more than you do. There'll be an inquest. It'll come out then."

Gray had to ask. "Are you comfortable with the outcome, Gracia?"

"Depends which one you mean? Am I comfortable with not having to go to the police? Yes. Am I comfortable with not being with Patrick any more? It's for the best, isn't it? I'm divorcing Claudio too, by the way, but you probably knew that. Having a bit of a clear-out, aren't I?"

Gray wanted to offer sympathy but she did not pause.

"Anyway, am I comfortable that one minute I was supposed to say one thing and then next minute something else? I mean, I suppose I get it. With Rob and everything. Patrick can't have been thinking straight, though it still seems a bit skewed. But yes, I suppose I'm comfortable, though it's a funny word."

"I'm sorry, Gracia," he ventured, "if you felt that I was not supportive."

"I think you were actually, in a way," she replied.

"Really?"

"Yeah. I mean being supportive and saying what someone wants to hear all the time aren't the same thing, are they? You're an honest man, Gray. You had to be true to yourself."

"Well, yes. Although in the end, I was never put to the test."

"What, you mean the police never contacted you?"

He related the tale of Malek's visit to his room at the RCJ. Gracia looked at him intently.

"And if Neil hadn't come in, and they'd asked the question ..?"

Her inquiry hung in the air for a moment.

"I'd have listened very carefully to the questions and answered truthfully. And then, I would have moved heaven and earth to ensure that you suffered no adverse consequences for being an innocent bystander, victim more like, who has to be cautious, always, about disclosing her presence, not for motives of personal gain or to avoid due process, but simply to protect her hard-earned and richly deserved professional reputation."

Gracia thought for a while. "Wow."

They fell to silence.

Gracia wiped a lump of bread around her plate. "I respect honesty, Gray."

"Of course you do." He was beginning to feel at ease.

"And," she continued, "I've got to say something, so I hope that you'll respect it too. You know, vice versa."

"I do. But this sounds dangerous?"

"It is," she continued, licking a garlicky finger and wiping her hand on the kitchen roll.

"Go on."

Gracia took a large mouthful of wine and placed her glass firmly on the table.

"Vanessa."

Gray braced himself.

"Yes?"

"Do you want to see her? I mean, nothing to do with me but she did dump you?"

Classic Gracia. Never shy of telling it how it was.

"Yes, I think I do."

A smile, as radiant as a hidden pearl, the more beautiful for its rarity.

"She was lovely, Gray. And she was good for you. So say yes. Now. Before she changes her mind. But," the smile faded, "I do have to be honest. I think there'll be a problem. A big problem."

Gray felt nervous. "Oh? Am I too old?"

"No, I don't think so?"

"Boring?"

"No."

"Set in my ways."

"A bit, but that's not it."

"Personal hygiene?"

"No, but you're getting closer."

"For heaven's sake Gracia, don't tell me I smell."

She laughed and shook her head.

"Don't worry."

"What the hell is it then?"

Gracia took another swig.

"You really want me to be honest?"

"Yes!" he almost shouted.

"I don't mean to be rude, Gray, but in my honest opinion you won't stand a cat's chance in hell with her if you turn up for your date in ANY of the clothes that are currently in your wardrobe which, basically, are exactly the same clothes as were in your wardrobe on the day you last saw her."

Gray laughed out loud. It was a joyful hee-hawing inhalation and exhalation. His face contracted into creases.

"It's true!" He gasped, mopping his eyes.

Gracia looked severe.

"You're going to have to do something. So, if you want my advice - to be fair, why would you? - but if you do I suggest you email her back, invite her somewhere very expensive but don't let her set eyes on you again till you and I have been shopping, OK?"

Gray looked at her, still smiling, shaking his head. "You're wicked, very wicked. You do know that?"

Gracia shrugged helplessly and gave a little nod of her head.

"Yeah. I know."

CONCLUSION

When stories end, characters live on. This is how they are progressing:

MR AL-SHAATER
Is now a leading expert in bowel surgery.

DC JAYNE SANDERS
Has left the police force to pursue her dream of becoming a professional distance runner. She regularly does training runs along the Regent's Canal.

DC JALAL MALEK
Is no longer a Detective Constable. He has been promoted to Detective Sergeant.

DS CARTWRIGHT
Has been dismissed from the Met after being found guilty of sexual misconduct with a junior officer.

PC BRIAN TEBBUTT
Has a young son who pesters him daily to buy a puppy. He refuses every time.

ROB KINGDOM
Has made a slow but complete recovery. He is in love with a girl he met at the gym which he religiously attends for rehab exercises. They plan to get married next year.

CHARLIE KINGDOM
The findings of the police were that the motorcyclist had been travelling at over 100 mph and not wearing a high visibility jacket at the time of the accident. In civil proceedings the case was settled on the basis of 50:50 liability. Both men were charged with causing serious injury by dangerous driving. In separate proceedings both pleaded guilty to the offence, were disqualified from driving and given suspended prison sentences.

   Charlie visited his brother every day in hospital for a month. He has left the estate agency and is now working for a mental health charity. He is in love with one of Rob's nurses and they are going out together.

THE MOTORCYCLIST
Made a full recovery and retained both legs. At his mother's insistence he sold his bike.

JENNY KINGDOM
Has become a volunteer at her local hospital where she makes delicious tea and fresh cakes for visitors. At home she is looking for wallpapers and fabrics with which to redecorate the boys' bedrooms.

JAMES MITCHELL
Continues to argue with his children and take interest in other people's affairs. His practice at the Bar is flourishing but, to his disappointment, he was not instructed to represent Charlie Kingdom.

ROSIE SHEEHAN
The talk on the canal is that she has gone back to Ireland.

GRACIA PEEL
Filming of the second series of *Initiate* took place in late May and June 2019. It aired on Netflix in April 2020 to critical acclaim. Gracia was the subject of very little publicity, as it was impossible to organise photo shoots during lockdown on account of the Covid-19 pandemic. She and Claudio are divorced. She has thrown away her black wig and dyed her hair red. The lead actor in *Initiate* says it suits her. He is five years older than Gracia and single. He has curly hair.

GRAY ANDREW
Updated his wardrobe. Vanessa has introduced him to her boys and they all get on well. She stays at Manchester Square when they are with their father and Gray usually stays with them once a week. He and Vanessa are planning a holiday in Provence.

His professional career is progressing well. He has become presiding judge of the northern circuit. He and Neil particularly enjoy staying in the Liverpool lodgings where he and Vanessa hosted a dinner in October 2019. Gracia attended. The chef, manager and waiting staff all asked for selfies to be taken with her.

PATRICK KINGDOM

Heard about the inquest into David McBrain's death from Emma Bromelow, a junior member of Chambers who was instructed by Camden Borough Council. She gave Patrick a summary of Rosie Sheehan's statement.

Camden Borough Council drew up a budget for repairs to the paving and kerbstones along the Regent's Canal but the work has yet to be carried out. Patrick has given up the flat in St John's Wood. He is now renting a two bedroomed flat in Pimlico which he shares with Charlie, whose office is in Victoria. Father and son regularly eat out together in London.

He spends as much time as possible working from home in West Haddon. Occasionally, in the evening, when they are sitting together watching the TV, he looks over to Jenny and smiles. She has suggested that they watch *Initiate* because someone at the hospital has told her it is really good. He says he doesn't think it would be his kind of thing.

AUTHOR'S NOTE

There are many people who have helped me during the creation of this book. In no particular order I thank Aimee-Lou Wood and Ralph Davis for their original walks and runs along the Regent's Canal during lockdown at the start of 2020 when I could not go there myself. Very sincere thanks to Dr Khalid Al-Hureibi for his expert advice on bowel surgery and to Detective Constable Suky Beard for her advice on police procedures, I am also indebted to Tamsin Courtenay and her book *Four Feet Under* which gives true and eye-opening accounts of rough sleepers' lives in and around London. I thank Kath Howell, Jose Hill, Sam Mainds, Kate Guild, Chris Bond, Ann Smith, Dominic Twose and Julie Day for their early readings and positive encouragement. I am also indebted to to Julie Day, Nicki Griffith and Paula Hubbard for painstaking proof reading and to Simon Dainty for putting my chaotic Word document into a book. I also thank Janet Laurence of Jericho Writers for her detailed reading of an early draft and for advice which, I know, led to improvements. In particular I thank my husband, Bill Davis who, as a High Court Judge with many years' experience of criminal and civil litigation gave me invaluable advice. As husband and captive audience I thank him for listening with creative interest to my musings on plot and character developments and for multiple readings. Every single one of these people has made invaluable contributions to this book.

While I was writing this book I was also learning how to become a runner. In order to place a punctuation mark within the process of developing both the book and my running I decided to run the 14.88 km length of the canal from Little Venice to Limehouse Basin in September 2020. In doing so I also raised money for St Mungo's, the London charity for the homeless. St Mungo's is a fabulous charity which does invaluable work. Please do read about it at www.stmungos.org.

To purchase copies of this book please contact the author via info@ginnydavis.com or ginnydavis2860@gmail.com

www.ginnydavis.com

ABOUT THE AUTHOR

Ginny Davis's career began as a translator of Spanish and French. She then became a barrister and practised in Birmingham. Her principal interest always lay in criminal law. When she became a mother, Ginny ceased practice and began her writing and performing career. She has written eleven plays. Six of these comprise the *Ruth Rich Saga*, a series of mostly one-woman comedies about modern family life. Her plays have sold out at the Edinburgh Fringe and in small and community venues throughout the UK. In 2016 she wrote *Learned Friends* which won Best Original Piece at Birminghamfest 2016 and was subsequently performed at Crown Court venues throughout the UK including London's Old Bailey.

Her plays *Hound Dog* and *The Mother in Law* and sketches *A Dog Walk* and *A Mum's Life* are published on a www.lazybeesscripts. co.uk.

As a writer of literature Ginny's career began when she won the Oundle Festival of Literature short story competition with *Requiem* in 2007. Her story *The Judge's Clerk* was shortlisted in the same competition the following year. *Near Chania* is published on www.pennyshorts.com. *What Lies Beneath the Surface* is her first full length novel.

She lives in Warwickshire with her husband. They have two adult children and a dog.

WHAT LIES BENEATH THE SURFACE

by Ginny Davis

Printed in Great Britain
by Amazon

17346199R00098